D0837533

THE UNIVERSE
ACCORDING TO
G. K. CHESTERTON

A Dictionary of the Mad,
Mundane and Metaphysical

G. K. CHESTERTON
With Illustrations by the Author

Edited by
DALE AHLQUIST

DOVER PUBLICATIONS, INC.
MINEOLA, NEW YORK

Contents

List of Illustrations

Introduction to the Dover Edition

Dale Ahlquist

> The heart of [Chesterton's] style is lucidity, produced by a complete
> rejection of ambiguity: complete exactitude of definition.
> —Hilaire Belloc, *On the Place of Gilbert Chesterton in English Letters*

In a lecture at Oxford in 1914, G. K. Chesterton talked about the word "romance." The modern world, he said, had lost the idea of what this word means. If an aged nobleman married a young lady in tights who danced in a chorus line, journalists—"who were subject to sudden fits of dementia"—would describe it in the papers as a "romantic" marriage. Ordinary people, he pointed out, really did marry for romantic reasons; there was plenty of romance in the plain towns of Tooting and Clapham, and he found it difficult to understand why his fellow journalists should reserve the word "romance" for the one instance in which the two people getting married had different but equally degraded motives. It was an example of how degraded a good word could become.

Chesterton then proceeded to define "romance." In literature, it was a mood that combined to the keenest extent the idea of danger and the idea of hope. The essence of romance was "adventure, and above all, unexpected success." It differed from tragedy in that it had from the very beginning the idea of hope; it differed from comedy in that it had from the beginning the idea of danger. "There must be courage in it, but the courage must not be mere fortitude, like that of Hector looking forward to his doom. And the courage must not be mere confidence, like that of Achilles driving all the Trojans before him. It must be a fighting chance."[1]

It is a shining, yet typical, example of Chesterton's poetic way of merely defining his terms before proceeding to his main argument. Though he is conventionally criticized as being paradoxical, and even sloppy and inattentive, as a writer, Chesterton is, on the contrary, razor sharp and radiantly lucid. The clarity of his thought is as astonishing as the vastness of his literary output. Though he seemingly writes about everything, he is always focused, always precise. It is difficult to force a different meaning onto something he says. It also is difficult to be ambiguous in one's own thinking afterwards. You have to do battle with the definitions he gives you.

H. I. Brock of the *New York Times* ventured to Beaconsfield, England, in 1912 to interview Chesterton. Brock, like many others, noted the comparison between Chesterton and the famous eighteenth-century man of letters, Dr. Samuel Johnson, who, like Chesterton, was a master essayist and a quotable commentator on the world around him. But Dr. Johnson was most famous for writing a dictionary; Chesterton never wrote a dictionary. In spite of this, Brock called him a lexicographer, "a twentieth century modification of the old dictionary maker—intent on putting words in their place."

The American reporter observed that Chesterton was constantly wrestling with the language, trying to express the clear idea and to extract truth from the raw material and muddled metaphors that had been handed down to him. "The trouble with words," Chesterton told his interviewer, "was that you had no sooner tacked one of them upon an observed fact—

merely as a label—than the word began to take charge, as it were, to usurp the place of the fact. So presently the fact was lost sight of and the word remained, saying sweeping and false things."[2]

We cannot fault Chesterton, who was always wrestling with words, for not writing a dictionary. He gave us one hundred books and hundreds of poems and at least five thousand essays on a myriad of topics. We are still very busy reading all that he wrote, and still tracking down *all* that he wrote. And yet, we wish he *had* written a dictionary. It would have been one of the great delights of twentieth-century literature, a book to open again and again and again, like any dictionary, only more so.

The connection between Chesterton and Dr. Johnson is pretty tight (in spite of the fact that the former failed to write a dictionary). Gilbert Keith Chesterton would often dress up to portray his literary predecessor. He also wrote an entertaining and provocative, though seldom performed, play called *The Judgment of Dr. Johnson*, in which the lines spoken by the title character contain both actual Johnson quotations and Chestertonian fabrications—the two are indistinguishable. In addition, Chesterton wrote introductions to books about Johnson, to new editions of his writings, and to a later edition of Boswell's classic *Life*. Perhaps the only other thing that separates Chesterton from Dr. Johnson is that Chesterton never had his own Boswell.

I might argue that Chesterton's greatest accomplishment was as a literary critic. He compares Johnson himself to a dictionary: "He took each thing, big or small, as it came. He told the truth, but on miscellaneous matters and in an accidental order." And, "he judged all things with a gigantic and detached good sense."[3] According to Chesterton, "a literary critic is permitted a greater levity."[4] There is levity in much of Johnson's *Dictionary*, and we see a similar levity in many of the definitions that Chesterton offers when he lays out his own terms. And this is the point of the present volume: even though G. K. Chesterton never explicitly wrote a dictionary, he explained his terms so explicitly in everything else he wrote, that he, in fact, wrote the *bones* of a dictionary, which we have reassembled here.

The first person to figure out that Chesterton was writing pieces of a dictionary was John Peterson, who started a newsletter in 1990 with the catchy title *Midwest Chesterton News*. It was a humble publication that would prove to be very fruitful, eventually giving birth to *Gilbert Magazine*, which has been called "the best magazine in the world."[5] John started a little feature in his newsletter called "Chesternitions," matching up Chesterton's definitions to the words he used, as he used them. I was immediately swept up by this idea, and, as I read Chesterton, I began circling the words that I noticed Chesterton would define as they cropped up. Nathan Allen joined in the chase, capturing a few good specimens as well. "Chesternitions" should be the name of this book because it is a perfect name for a Chesterton dictionary, and it is just a great word. Chesternitions. [It makes you wonder why the publisher didn't agree to it. Must be neologophobia: a fear of new words.]

In any case, this book has been many years in the making. First of all, it is compiled from thirty-six years of Chesterton's published writing, the first third of the twentieth century. Then, the compiling itself took about twenty years. And we have only begun. We still haven't gotten serious about it. There is a much larger Chesterton dictionary to be created.

Dr. Johnson's dictionary had 2,300 pages and 43,000 entries. I'm not saying that we could equal that accomplishment, but if we did some more work mining Chesterton's writings, which are in excess of sixteen million words, we could come up with a much more substantial Chester-lexicon than the present effort. The more that I have worked on this project, the more I am convinced that Chesterton *could* have written a dictionary. His vivid descriptions of ideas, his clear explanations of what he means, his poetic renderings of words, not only leave us wanting more, but heavily hint that there *is* more.

Some of his definitions are satirical, but never really coldly sarcastic, as in Ambrose Bierce's *Devil's Dictionary*. In fact, *The Universe According to G. K. Chesterton* is, in many respects, the counterpart, or even the antidote, to *The Devil's Dictionary*. Chesterton's philosophy is one of hope, not despair. While Bierce scoffs at sacred beliefs, Chesterton skewers skepticism with a very sharp sword. He scoffs at the scoffers. He also draws his strength from tradition and has very little faith in fashion.

Frequently occurring words in Chesterton's writings produce multiple definitions that reinforce each other. But some of his richest definitions are his shortest: *conclude* is "to shut up," *corruption* is "death from within." Chesterton can pack huge meanings into a minimum of words. That is what poets do.

These are not dull and detached definitions. They are not neutral, but neither are they narrow and purely subjective. There really are no neutral words. Every word is full of meaning that is connected to the larger meaning of things. Chesterton's definitions are defensible even if they can be disagreed with, as they most certainly will be. But a man who takes a position cannot take it ambiguously. Nor can he take it dishonestly. As Chesterton explains:

> It is true of almost anything that he who defends it defines it. Defense involves definition either in conducting a controversy or constructing a fort. The wall round a city is not merely a precaution against the city

being destroyed; it is also the process by which the city is created. This is the truth of psychology which really feeds the passion of patriotism, and even of militant patriotism. The things we love, the things we think beautiful, are things of a certain shape which we recognize.[6]

Each of Chesterton's definitions, like any other definition, hangs on the word "is." Every definition is stating that one thing is something else, even though it is itself, not something else. There is a paradox here. We are trying to understand a word using other words. When defining a word, we are forced to use different words than the word we are defining. It does no good, as it were, to call a spade a spade. There is not, as Chesterton says, "any kind of logical or philosophical use in merely saying the same word twice over."[7]

It is a further paradox that some of the simplest things are most difficult to define. The simple things are not simple. The most basic words are extremely subtle and complex and tend to be larger than our understanding of them. The challenge of the lexicographer is to rein in these wild beasts. Not only to rein them in, but pen them in. Chesterton says, "to define a thing is literally and grammatically to limit it,"[8] and thus to define *art* or *God* is "to limit the illimitable," which seems rather impossible. (Yet you will find Chesternitions of these words.) Chesterton himself admits that the one unbearable insult to the divine order is "the insult that it is very easily explained after all."[9]

To further complicate matters, we are using a decaying language to define these words. We suffer from "that perpetual degeneration of words which is the whole history of human language."[10] It is a dilemma that Chesterton claims is indicative of "the restlessness and fugitive quality of our time."[11]

Chesterton considers himself a collector of catchwords, much as a butterfly collector tries to pin down those things that flutter past. The difference is that catchwords are more like moths than like butterflies; that is, they corrupt and destroy. Catchwords, says Chesterton, are used as "a substitute for thinking,"[12] and come to mean the very opposite of what the words themselves ought to mean. For example, Chesterton catches his friend H. G. Wells using a catchword when he says that we need "a restatement of religious truth." But Chesterton knows that this is not what Wells really means:

> To restate a thing is to state it over again; possibly to state the thing in other words, but to state the same thing. It is nonsense to say that the statement, "The dog is mad," is restated in the amended form, "The cow is dead"; and it is equally absurd that the news that the devil is dead should be called a restatement of the tradition that the devil is dangerous. In truth, as I have said, these people really mean the very reverse of what they say. They do not mean that we are to take the same idea and restate it in new words. On the contrary, they mean that we are to use the old words and attach to them a new idea.[13]

Chesterton tries hard to avoid "logomachy," which is "that mere quarrel about a word."[14] A quarrel differs from an argument in that an argument is productive to the point of ending in agreement, whereas a quarrel is simply wearisome and endless. But the reason we quarrel instead of arguing is that we do not define our terms. We use fewer and fewer words and force them to mean more and more. But the practical result is that we have less and less to say. Not only does this cause one of our "chief troubles at present," namely, "that words and things do not fit each other,[15] but it reflects another problem: Our sloppy and lazy way of speaking leads to sloppy and lazy thinking. And vice versa. "It is difficult to believe," observes Chesterton, "that people who are obviously careless about language can really be very careful about anything else."[16]

Chesterton complains of the "confusion into which our modern thought has fallen; confusion not I mean merely as to original theories or ultimate conclusions, but confusion about categories and the mere nature of logical terms."[17] And so Chesterton has chosen to fight this confusion: "I deal with the use and abuse of logic; the use and abuse of language; the duty of talking sense even on the wrong side; the duty of not talking nonsense even on the right side. There may be things I think so absolutely abnormal as to deserve to be treated as monstrosities."[18]

We need to agree even to disagree. We need to have some common ground in order to argue. We must start with some agreement so that we can have a fruitful disagreement. We must begin then, by defining our terms.

In the pages that follow, you will find words defined in a way to delight and perhaps jolt you. In addition to common words, there will be a few uncommon words, and even a few terms that were not used in Chesterton's time, but for which he still managed to anticipate a definition. For extra spice, there is a sprinkling of unique words that are Chesterton's own inventions. The sources given are the chapter titles from books by Chesterton, books by others to which Chesterton contributed a chapter or an introduction, and periodicals that featured a literary essay by Chesterton. There are also some selections from the two Maisie Ward biographies of Chesterton. The dates of the *Illustrated London News* are from the American edition, which, until 1913, were two weeks later than the English edition. If the references are not precise enough for some scholars, they will have to settle for the precision of the definitions themselves. The only reference they will need is this book, which by all rights, should be a standard reference work for years to come. I am not saying this to boast of anything that I have done, because the accomplishment is not mine; it is

G. K. Chesterton's—he is not only Dr. Johnson's rightful heir as a lexicographer extraordinaire, but a walking and talking gift to the English language. It is a privilege to help his words live on after him.

Notes

1. *Manchester Guardian*, May 18, 1914.

2. *The New York Times*, Aug. 18, 1912.

3. "Dr. Johnson," *GKC as MC*, 1929.

4. Introduction to Vol. IV, *The Life Of Samuel Johnson,* by James Boswell, Doubleday, Page and Co., Garden City, N.Y., 1922.

5. by me.

6. *Century*, March, 1923.

7. "Dombey and Son," *Appreciations and Criticisms of the Works of Charles Dickens, 1911.*

8. *Daily News*, February 7, 1902.

9. *Ibid.*

10. *Illustrated London News,* December 9, 1905.

11. *Illustrated London News,* December 24, 1910.

12. *Illustrated London News,* January 14, 1928.

13. *Illustrated London News,* June 9, 1928.

14. "The Hound of Heaven," *The Common Man*, 1950.

15. *Ibid.*

16. *Illustrated London News*, April 4, 1908.

17. *Daily News*, April 14, 1906.

18. *Illustrated London News*, February 20, 1932.

G. K. Chesterton on Definitions

Definitions are very dreadful things: they do the two things that most men, especially comfortable men, cannot endure. They fight; and they fight fair. ("The Church of the Servile State," *Utopia of Usurers*)

To define a thing is literally and grammatically to limit it. (*Daily News*, Feb. 7, 1902)

I have generally found dictionary definitions extraordinarily bad. (*Illustrated London News*, Jan. 8, 1927)

The word that has no definition is the word that has no substitute. ("The Dickens Period," *Charles Dickens*)

For it is generally difficult to destroy, or even to defy, a thing that we cannot define. (*Illustrated London News*, June 8, 1929)

The mere meaning of words is now strangely forgotten and falsified. ("The Chartered Libertine," *A Miscellany of Men*)

For in truth I believe that the only way to say anything definite is to define it, and all definition is by limitation and exclusion; and that the only way to say something distinct is to say something distinguishable; and distinguishable from everything else. In short, I think that a man does not know what he is saying until he knows what he is not saying. (*Illustrated London News*, Dec. 15, 1934)

If once we begin to quibble and quarrel about what words ought to mean, or can be made to mean, we shall find ourselves in a mere world of words, most wearisome to those who are concerned with thoughts. ("The Hound of Heaven," *The Common Man*)

I have dared to go in for definitions. (*Illustrated London News*, Jan. 3, 1914)

Chesternitions: A Chesterton Dictionary

A

abortion: the mutilation of womanhood and the massacre of men unborn. ("The Meanness of the Motive," *Eugenics and Other Evils*)

absent-minded: good-natured. ("The Six Philosophers," *The Man Who Was Thursday*)

absent-mindedness: present-mindedness on something else. ("Another Fantastic Suburb," *Return to Chesterton*)

actor: a bundle of masks. ("The Paradise of Thieves," *The Wisdom of Father Brown*)

addiction: the point where the one incidental form of pleasure, which comes from a certain article of consumption, becomes more important than all the vast universe of natural pleasure, which it finally destroys. ("Lunacy and Letters," *Lunacy and Letters*)

adventure: an inconvenience rightly considered. ("On Running After One's Hat," *All Things Considered*)

advertisement: temptation; a loud evasion used in favor of bad wine and bad milk; the windy weakness of vanity; an attack upon the eyes and ears, the senses and the soul; rich people asking for more money. (*The Temptation of St. Anthony*;

3

Illustrated London News, June 30, 1928, Feb. 6, 1926; *G.K.'s Weekly*, Aug. 7, 1926; "The Philosophy of Sightseeing," *The New Jerusalem*)

aesthete: an erotomaniac; a man whose pleasures are principally in artistic feeling; the mild man who matches a russet waistcoat with olive trousers, rather than the man (perhaps the equally lovely man) who matches a golden waistcoat with crimson trousers; a man who aims at harmony rather than beauty. If his hair does not match the mauve sunset against which he is standing, he hurriedly dyes his hair another shade of mauve. If his wife does not go with the wallpaper, he gets a curtain or a divorce. ("The Miser and his Friends," *A Miscellany of Men*; *Illustrated London News*, Dec. 25, 1909)

aesthetic: a certain type or tint of beauty—the somewhat mixed, melancholy, and tentative; the arrangement of effects rather than the primary creation of them. (*Illustrated London News*, Dec. 25, 1909)

agnostic: one whose dogma is that there is no dogma. ("Ibsen," *A Handful of Authors*)

agnosticism: the ancient confession of ignorance; a decision in favor of indecision; the more priggish form of humility; the negative side of mysticism. ("The Myth of the Mayflower," *Fancies vs. Fads*; *America*, Oct. 11, 1930; *Daily News*, Nov. 2, 1912; "The Puritan," *George Bernard Shaw*)

alcohol: our general word for the essence of wine and beer and such things, that comes from a people (the Arabs) who have made a war upon them. ("Wine When it is Red," *All Things Considered*)

alphabet: a set of symbols, like heraldry. (*Illustrated London News*, Nov. 20, 1915)

AESTHETE

amateur: a man who loves a thing so much that he not only practices it without any hope of fame or money, but even practices it without any hope of doing it well, who must love the toils of the work more than any other man can love the rewards of it. ("Browning and His Marriage," *Robert Browning*)

America: the land of Edison and quick lunches. (*Illustrated London News*, Feb. 10, 1906)

American: a curious compound of impudence and sensitiveness. ("The Strange Crime of John Boulnois," *The Wisdom of Father Brown*)

amusement: a narcotic. (*Illustrated London News*, May 3, 1930)

anachronism: the pedantic word for eternity; an artistic truth that telescopes time and history together. (*Illustrated London News*, Dec. 25, 1926)

anarchist: a man who will not accept any authority, who treats the community around him as something to which he does not belong. (*Daily News*, Jan. 21, 1911)

anarchy: the perpetual doing of small, indefensible things; that condition of mind or methods in which you cannot stop yourself; the loss of that self-control which can return to the normal. (*Illustrated London News*, Nov. 21, 1908; "The Anarchy from Above," *Eugenics and Other Evils*)

anger: knowing what you don't want more than what you do. (*Century Magazine*, Nov. 1912)

Anglo-Saxon: a race that is an entire myth, that not only has no existence, but has not even any very lucid verbal meaning. (*Daily News*, April 14, 1906)

anti-sentimentalism: a rather priggish and a rather snobbish form of sentimentalism. (*Illustrated London News*, Aug. 20, 1927)

anthropologist: a student of prehistoric man who has his own stone axe to grind. (*Illustrated London News*, Sept. 10, 1927)

anthropology: the study of anthropoids; the disproportionate disposition, in popular science, to turn the study of human beings into the study of savages. ("The Permanent Philosophy," *St. Thomas Aquinas*)

anthropomorphism: the notion that primitive men attributed phenomena to a god in human form in order to explain them, because his mind in its sullen limitation could not reach any further than his own clownish existence. ("Science and the Savages," *Heretics*)

architecture: the most practical and the most dangerous of the arts; the alphabet of giants; the largest system of symbols ever made to meet the eyes of men; the art of putting buildings together so that they will stand up and even stand still; the most arresting and obvious of the denials which the higher reason really offers to the merely evolutionary vision of formlessness and change; the most solid and striking assertion of man's sublime ambition of finality. (BBC talk, Jan. 1933; *Illustrated London News*, July 19, 1924; Feb.14, 1925)

argument: differing in order to agree; the most dazzling and delightful of all human games. (*Illustrated London News*, April 1, 1911; *Daily News*, Nov. 18, 1901)

aristocracy: the governing class governed by a perfectly simple principle of keeping all the important things to themselves, and giving the papers and the people unimportant things to discuss; the drift or slide of men into a sort of natural pomposity and praise of the powerful, which is the most

ANTHROPOLOGY

easy and obvious affair in the world; a priesthood without a god. (*Illustrated London News*, Mar. 15, 1930; "The Eternal Revolution," *Orthodoxy*; "The Mirror of Christ," *St. Francis of Assisi*)

art: the signature of man; a symbol that expresses very real spiritualities under the surface of life; a thing of glimpses. ("The Man in the Cave," "Man and Mythologies," *The Everlasting Man*; "The Domesticity of Detectives," *The Uses of Diversity*, "Ibsen," *A Handful of Authors*)

artist: a person of exquisite susceptibilities; the man who is able to say what everyone else means; a person who can get good out of wine without even drinking it, or out of gold without ever spending it; a person who communicates something. He may communicate it more or less quickly; he may communicate it to a smaller or larger number of people. But it is a question of communication and not merely of what some people call expression. Or rather, strictly speaking, unless it is communication it is not expression. ("The Secret of a Train," *Tremendous Trifles*; *The Observer*, Feb. 26, 1911; *Illustrated London News*, Oct 17, 1925; Nov. 27, 1926)

artistic: to have the intellect and all its instruments on the spot and ready to go to the point. ("The Domesticity of Detectives," *The Uses of Diversity*)

asceticism: the appetite for what one does not like; in the religious sense, the repudiation of the great mass of human joys because of the supreme joyfulness of the one joy, the religious joy; the idea that truth alone is satisfying. ("Prologue," *Four Faultless Felons*; "Francis," *Varied Types*)

assumption: something you do not doubt. You can, of course, if you like, doubt the assumption at the beginning of your argument, but in that case you are beginning a different argument with another assumption at the beginning of it. Every argument begins with an infallible dogma; and that infallible dogma can only be disputed by falling back on some other infallible dogma; you can never prove your first statement, or it would not be your first. (*Daily News*, June 22, 1907)

astrology: the view that the stars are personal beings, governing our lives. ("The Aristotelian Revolution," *St. Thomas Aquinas*)

Atheism: the reversal of a subconscious assumption in the soul, the sense that there is a meaning and a direction in the world it sees; the notion of impersonal power; the most daring of all dogmas for it is the assertion of a universal negative. ("The End of the World," *The Everlasting Man*; *Illustrated London News*, Dec. 2, 1916; "Charles II," *Twelve Types*)

atheist: a man limited and constrained by his own logic to a very sad simplification; a man who is not interested in anything except attacks on atheism. ("Babies and Distributism," "Frozen Free Thought," *The Well and the Shallows*)

authority: that which is necessary for the granting of liberties: e.g., man is free, not because there is no God, but because he needs a God to set him free. By authority he is free. ("The Chartered Libertine," *A Miscellany of Men*)

automobile: a way of going very quickly when I am bored in London to bore somebody else in Yorkshire. (*Daily News*, Jan. 5, 1907)

axiom: a first principle which is unproved but which begins all proofs. (*Illustrated London News*, July 10, 1915)

B

baby: the Kingdom of God; the most beautiful thing on earth. ("The Orthodox Barber," *Tremendous Trifles*; "Christianity and Rationalism," *The Clarion*, 1904)

baptism: birth through a Holy Spirit. ("The Paradoxes of Christianity," *Orthodoxy*)

barbarian: the enemy of civilization, willfully at war with the principles by which human society has been made possible hitherto; the man who cannot love—no, nor even hate—his neighbor as himself; the man who does not believe in chivalry in war or charity in peace; and, above all, who does not believe in modesty in anything. Whatever he does, he overdoes. ("The War on the Word," "The Refusal of Reciprocity," *The Appetite of Tyranny*; *Illustrated London News*, July 31, 1920)

barbarism: the destruction of all that men have ever understood, by men who do not understand it. (*Illustrated London News*, Aug. 5, 1933)

barber: a member of that stern, rugged, heroic race that exists to tell men of their baldness, as priests to tell them of their sins. (*Illustrated London News*, Apr. 24, 1909)

beer: primarily a liquid refreshment for the quenching of thirst; and our fathers thought no more of the peril of its slight stimulation than we think of the peril of the slight nervous effect of tea. In Bavaria, where nobody ever dreamed that beer could be forbidden, beer is a very light and mild brew shared by husbands, wives and children in harmless picnics. In Chicago, where beer is forbidden, beer has acted as a sort of dynamite of revolution and has turned a racketeer into a dictator. (*Illustrated London News*, Mar. 24, 1923; Aug. 1, 1931)

beauty: precise proportion. (*Illustrated London News*, May 31, 1924)

beggar: someone who is manifestly sent by heaven to make the comfortable classes uncomfortable; a man who offers you the opportunity to fulfill your own ideals; any person, in any position, who has nothing but thanks to give for a service. ("The Return of the Romans," *The Resurrection of Rome*; *Illustrated London News*, Feb. 25, 1911)

Bible: the strange small book from which all Christianity came. ("Authority and the Adventurer," *Orthodoxy*)

Big Ben: the arrogant clock-tower of Parliament. ("The Eye of Apollo," *The Innocence of Father Brown*)

bigotry: an incapacity to conceive seriously the alternative to a proposition; the anger of men who have no opinions. ("The Bigot," *Lunacy and Letters*; "Concluding Remarks," *Heretics*)

biology: the history of animals, and especially of the uniformity of animals. (*Illustrated London News*, Jan. 22, 1921)

birth control: less birth and no control; a scheme for preventing birth in order to escape control. ("Obstinate Orthodoxy," *The Thing*; "The Surrender upon Sex," *The Well and the Shallows*)

birthday: a glorification of the idea of life. (*Illustrated London News*, Nov. 28, 1908)

blackmail: the most morbid of human things because it is a crime concealing a crime; a black plaster on a blacker wound. ("The Absence of Mr. Glass," *The Wisdom of Father Brown*)

blasphemy: regarding in a commonplace manner something which other and happier people regard in a rapturous and imaginative manner; the cold contempt for God; trying to say (at the same time) that God does not exist, and that He ought to be ashamed of existing, or possibly that he ought to be ashamed of not existing; an artistic effect that depends on belief. (If any one doubts this, let him sit down seriously and try to think blasphemous thoughts about Thor. I think his family will find him at the end of the day in a state of some exhaustion.); taking things too lightly. (*William Blake*; *Dublin Review*, Jan.–Mar., 1935; The End of the Moderns," *The Common Man*; "Introductory Remarks," *Heretics*; "A Plea for Hasty Journalism," *The Apostle and the Wild Ducks*)

booing: boisterous interruptions of art. (*Daily News*, Nov. 19, 1904)

book: a sacred object. ("Lunacy and Letters," *Lunacy and Letters*)

Bohemian: the eccentric or slovenly or straggling camp of followers of the arts, who exhibit dubious manners and dubious morals. ("Browning in Italy," *Robert Browning*)

Bolshevist: a man who has taken this transcendental truth of human equality from the people who knew what it really meant, and proceeded to act on the assumption that it must be true and that it must not be transcendental. (*G.K.'s Weekly*, Oct. 16, 1926)

boredom: irreverence for the present; the next condition to death. (*Illustrated London News,* July 30, 1930; "A Defence of Bores," *Lunacy and Letters*)

bridge: a road across a river; that which springs out with wings of stone into the void and takes hold on a new land. (*New Witness,* June 14, 1918; *Illustrated London News,* Aug. 24, 1912)

broadminded: living on prejudices and never looking at them. (*Illustrated London News,* May 5, 1928)

bully: the man who acts on the assumption that he will not have to fight. (*Daily News*, Dec. 12, 1908)

bureaucracy: the system based on the idea that all men must be so stupid that they cannot manage their own affairs and also so clever that they can manage each other's. (*Illustrated London News*, Sept. 27, 1919)

business: militarism without the military virtues. ("The Drift from Domesticity," *The Thing*)

businessman: the middle man. (*New Witness*, Jan. 6, 1916)

C

cad: a man who cannot be courteous even when he tries to be. (*Illustrated London News*, Oct. 3, 1914)

Calvinism: a very cruel form of fatalism; the most non-Christian of Christian systems. ("The Outline of Liberty," *The Common Man*; "The Vengeance of the Flesh," *Eugenics and Other Evils*)

Calvinist: a Catholic whose imagination had been in some way caught and overpowered by the one isolated theological truth of the power and knowledge of God; and he offered to it human sacrifice, not only of every human sentiment, but of every other divine quality. ("The Idols of Scotland," *The Thing*)

camel: the enormous unnatural friend of man; the prehistoric pet. He is never known to have been wild and might make a man fancy that all wild animals had once been tame. ("The Other Side of the Desert," *The New Jerusalem*)

camouflage: in the art of war, to paint things with invisibility; in the art of peace, a French word for humbug. (*Century Magazine*, Dec. 1922)

campaigning: electioneering; endless self-gratification and self-display. (*G.K.'s Weekly*, Aug. 15, 1935)

cannibalism: eating boiled missionary; a religious exercise, and, like most religious exercises, highly distasteful and frequently neglected. ("The Roots of Sanity," *The Thing*; *Illustrated London News*, Aug. 19, 1911)

cant: something that has been said once too often. (*Illustrated London News*, July 30, 1927)

Capitalism: the commercial system in which supply immediately answers to demand, and in which everybody seems to be thoroughly dissatisfied and unable to get anything he wants; the economic system that has to keep the poor man just stout enough to do the work and just thin enough to have to do it; the dispossession of the population of all forms of real productive property. ("How to Write a Detective Story," *The Spice of Life*; "Science and the Eugenists," *Utopia of Usurers*; "Last Turn," *The Well and the Shallows*)

caricature: comic congruity; the art of the grotesque. (*Illustrated London News*, Dec. 25, 1926)

cathedral: a leap of live stone like a frozen fountain. (*Illustrated London News*, July 30, 1910)

Catholic Church: the one supremely inspiring and irritating institution in the world; the only thing that saves a man from the degrading slavery of being a child of his age. ("The Case of Spain," *The Well and the Shallows*; "Why I am a Catholic," *The Thing*)

Catholicism: to a Catholic, a view of the universe satisfying all sides of life; a complete and complex truth with something to say about everything; a balance made of definitions that correct each other and to some seem to contradict each other. ("The Demons and the Philosophers," *The Everlasting Man*; *Superstitions of the Sceptic*)

centralization: the great modern convenience and the great modern inconvenience. (*Illustrated London News*, Jan. 9, 1926)

ceremonial: physical and visible symbols of belief. (*Daily News*, Oct. 24, 1903)

ceremony: acted poetry. (*Illustrated London News*, June 2, 1928)

chair: the noble wooden quadruped on which I sit, four extra wood legs besides the two given me by the gods. ("On Being Moved," *Lunacy and Letters*)

chaos: formless nothing. (*New York American*, April 1, 1933)

charity: a reverent agnosticism towards the complexity of the soul; an ideal that exists wholly for the undeserving; loving the unlovable. ("Paganism and Mr. Lowes Dickinson," *Heretics*)

charlatan: one sufficiently dignified to despise the tricks that he employs. ("Oscar Wilde," *A Handful of Authors*)

child: somebody you can play with; the explanation of the ancient ties connecting the father and mother. (*Magic,* Act II; Part 5, *The Superstition of Divorce*)

childhood: that godlike time when we can act stories, be our own heroes, and at the same instant dance and dream. ("The Tremendous Adventure of Major Brown," *The Club of Queer Trades*)

CHILDHOOD

childish: full of energy, but without an idea of independence; fundamentally as eager for authority as for information and butterscotch. ("The Dreadful Duty of Gudge," *What's Wrong with the World*)

childlike: seeing everything with a simple pleasure, even the complex things. ("On Sandals and Simplicity," *Heretics*)

children: human beings who are allowed to do what everyone else really desires to do, as for instance, to fly kites, or when seriously wronged to emit prolonged screams for several minutes. ("The Philosophy of Islands," *The Spice of Life*)

chivalry: a reverence for weakness; Christian courage; a disdain of death; the moral attitude of a man with his back to the wall. ("The Way of the Desert," *The New Jerusalem*; "The Paradoxes of Christianity," *Orthodoxy*; "The End of the World," *The Everlasting Man*)

Christian Science: the direct denial both of science and of Christianity. ("Unknown America," *Sidelights*)

Christianity: the belief that a certain human being whom we call Christ stood to a certain superhuman Being whom we call God in a certain unique transcendental relation which we call sonship. (*Daily News*, Dec. 19, 1903)

Christmas: the celestial paradox of the birthday of God. (*New Witness*, July 15, 1917)

Church: a humble effort to utter God. ("A Circle of Friends," *Gilbert Keith Chesterton*)

cinema: a central mechanism for unrolling certain regular patterns called pictures, expressing the most vulgar millionaires' notion of the taste of the most vulgar millions. ("Babies and Distributism," *The Well and the Shallows*)

citizen: an advisor of the nation. (*Illustrated London News* June 12, 1909)

civilized man: someone who, like the religious man, recognizes the strange and irritating fact that something exists besides himself. ("Arms and the Armistice," *The End of the Armistice*)

civilization: the storied tower we have erected to affront nature; that self-command by which man can revert to the normal. ("A Scandal in the Village," *The Ball and the Cross*; *Illustrated London News*, Nov. 23, 1912)

classic: a book which can be praised without being read and quoted instead of being read; a king who may now be deserted, but who cannot now be dethroned. (*Illustrated London News*, May 11, 1907; June 5, 1926; "The Dickens Period," *Charles Dickens*)

cliché: a catchword or phrase that has no second meaning, and soon loses its first meaning; a phrase which everybody speaks and nobody hears. (*Illustrated London News*, May 13, 1932; Aug. 31, 1929)

clouds: the colossal cumuli that tumble about like a celestial pillow-fight. ("The Republic of Peaceways," *The Flying Inn*)

cocktail: the coward's drink; perhaps the only practical product of Prohibition. ("The Cowardice of Cocktails," *Sidelights*)

coercion: the first essential element in government. ("The Brand of the Fleur-de-lis," *What's Wrong with the World*)

coincidence: a spiritual pun. ("An Example and a Question," *Irish Impressions*)

Collectivism: trying to remedy the monstrous concentration of wealth by more concentration of wealth into the central and final concentration of it; a cold administration by quite detached officials. (*Daily News*, Feb. 17, 1902; "Conclusion," *What's Wrong with the World*)

commercialism: the art of arresting the attention without awakening the mind. ("How to Write a Detective Story," *The Spice of Life*)

common sense: an extinct branch of psychology; a sense of reality common to all; a sensibility duly distributed in all normal directions; the power of preserving our real impressions undistorted and intact; an instinct for the probable. ("The Unpsychological Age," *Sidelights*; "The Return to Religion," *The Well and the Shallows*; "Dickens and America," *Charles Dickens*; *Daily News*, Feb. 18, 1902; "Professors and Prehistoric Men," *The Everlasting Man*)

Communism: the system that reforms the pickpocket by forbidding pockets; the Franciscan Movement without the moderating balance of the Church; the Soul of the Hive; the child and heir of Capitalism. ("The Beginning of the Quarrel," *The Outline of Sanity*; "Why I am a Catholic," *The Thing*; "The Aristotelian Revolution," *St. Thomas Aquinas*; *Illustrated London News*, July 20, 1935)

competition: fierce and ruthless imitation; a furious plagiarism. (*Daily News*, July 24, 1902; "The Great Dickens Characters," *Charles Dickens*)

compulsion: the highly modern mark of a great many modern things—compulsory education, compulsory insurance, compulsory temperance, and soon, perhaps, compulsory arbitration. (*Illustrated London News*, June 5, 1920)

compulsory education: a system, the purpose of which is to deprive common people of their common sense. (*Illustrated London News*, Sep. 7, 1929)

comradeship: the club; a certain cool and casual association which is mostly masculine and which is always pluralist. (*Illustrated London News*, June 12, 1909)

conclude: to shut up. ("Why I am a Catholic," *The Thing*)

confession: facing the reality about oneself. ("The God with the Golden Key," *Autobiography*)

conscience: that signal to the soul that all of us must obey; the voice of God, or at the least the moral sense of mankind, of which the whole point is that it is universal. (*America,* Jan. 4, 1930; *Illustrated London News*, June 2, 1917)

Conservative: a man who wishes to keep his money. (*Daily News*, Sept. 8, 1906)

Constitution: simply the statement of how laws are made. It has no business whatever with saying which laws should be made, still less with saying that one particularly silly law must never be unmade. (*Illustrated London News*, June 28, 1928)

conversation: the one instance of successful collaboration. (*Daily News*, Sept. 13, 1905)

contentment: being pleased, placidly, perhaps, but still positively pleased; the power of getting out of any situation all that there is in it. ("The Contented Man," *A Miscellany of Men*)

continuity: a series of restorations. (*Illustrated London News*, Nov. 19, 1910)

contraception: love towards sex that is *not* towards life. (*G.K.'s Weekly*, Mar. 28, 1925)

controversial: expressing opinions that are widely controverted. Whether what we say to somebody is provocative or no does not depend on ourselves; it does not depend even on what we say; it depends upon whom we say it to. (*Illustrated London News*, August 14, 1926)

controversy: the pure art of positive challenge, of sudden repartee, of pugnacious and exasperating query. ("Martin Chuzzlewit," *Appreciations*)

convention: a coming together; getting people to act alike; the meeting place of the emotions of myriads of men; the common soul of the crowd. (*Illustrated London News*, June 4, 1910; July 25, 1931; "The Philosopher," *George Bernard Shaw*)

corruption: death from within. (*Daily News*, Oct. 17, 1908)

cosmopolitan: strictly, that a man is a citizen of the Cosmos; that the stars are his street lamps, and the sea his reservoir; that he walks familiarly under a law common to all things. But the man who calls himself, as a rule, a cosmopolitan, is precisely the man who never is like this. The cosmopolitan never lives in the Cosmos. He is a globe-trotter that never sees the globe. He is the very reverse of a patriot. He is a philanderer of the nations. (*Daily News*, June 30, 1904; "Elizabeth Barrett Browning," *Varied Types*; "On Mr. Rudyard Kipling," *Heretics*)

courage: a strong desire to live taking the form of a readiness to die. ("The Paradoxes of Christianity," *Orthodoxy*)

courtesy: the wedding of humility and dignity. ("A Grammar of Knighthood," *The Well and the Shallows*)

craftsmanship: the almost unconscious touch of art upon all necessary things. ("The Rebellion of the Rich," *A Short History of England*)

cramming: the tendency of a man to give everything to what he is studying except time and patience and reverence. It is a great mistake to suppose that people only cram for examinations; they cram for culture, they cram for success in life, they cram for Imperial wars, and morally and spiritually speaking, they cram for the Day of Judgment. (*Daily News*, Oct. 10, 1901)

crank: a man who always manages (by an eternal crisis of self-consciousness) to combine all the disadvantages of everything; the man who is always solving what is solved already; a man who knows his case and yet does not really know his subject, who is well-read, but not widely read; the sort of man who writes letters to the newspaper, which generally do not appear in the newspaper, but which do appear afterwards as pamphlets, printed (or misprinted) at his own expense, and circulated to a hundred wastepaper baskets. (*Illustrated London News*, July 19, 1913; *G.K.'s Weekly*, April 26, 1934; *New York American*, May 20, 1933; "The Quick One," *The Scandal of Father Brown*)

creation: turning anything into something. (*Daily News*, April 26, 1905)

creative: some image evoked by the individual imagination which might never have been evoked by any other imagination, and adds something to the imagery of the world. (*Illustrated London News*, April 11, 1931)

creed: the sword of the spirit, the only tool with which the mind can fight. (*Daily News*, June 26, 1909)

criticism: words about words. ("The Strangest Story in the World," *The Everlasting Man*)

critics: analysts of pleasure, who should justify to the public its own feelings in the act of justifying their own. (*Illustrated London News*, Nov. 20, 1909)

Cross: that terrible tree which was the death of God and the life of man; the symbol of Christianity that has a contradiction at its center and stretches its four arms forever without losing its shape. ("Man and Mythologies," *The Everlasting Man*; "The Maniac," *Orthodoxy*)

culture: the art of growing things; the mental thrift of our fathers; knowing the best that has been said but also knowing the best that has been done, and even doing our best to do it; the healthy growing of ideas from their own original seed. And if you don't like that, you don't like civilization. Also, it does not like you. (*Illustrated London News*, Nov. 6, 1920; "Is Humanism a Religion?" *The Thing*; "The English Peasant," *GKC as MC*; *Illustrated London News*, Nov. 9, 1912)

curiosity: a mere appetite for truth. (*Illustrated London News*, July 25, 1914)

cynic: a man who is flippant about serious things. ("Mark Twain," *A Handful of Authors*)

cynicism: that condition of mind in which we hold that life is in its nature mean and arid, that no soul contains genuine goodness, and no state of things genuine reliability; a restless kind of shame; a certain corrupt fatigue about human affairs. ("Browning in Later Life," *Robert Browning*; *Illustrated London News*, Dec. 20, 1919; "The Progressive," *George Bernard Shaw*)

D

damn: the most famous of all words of one syllable. (*Illustrated London News*, June 5, 1909)

dancing: the act of moving one's limbs to music. (*Illustrated London News,* Aug. 25 1906)

danger: death from without. (*Daily News*, Oct. 17, 1908)

Dark Ages: Something that was not so much Rome as the long, fantastic shadow flung by her towers at sunset that fell across the whole earth. (*Illustrated London News*, Nov. 13, 1920)

Darwinism: biological conjecture for overcoming some difficulties in the very ancient doctrine of evolution; a scientific excuse for moral anarchy. (*Daily News*, June 26, 1909; *Illustrated London News,* May 29, 1920)

death: the most obvious and universal fact, but also the least agreeable one; a distinctly exciting moment; a positive and defined condition, but it belongs entirely to the dead person. (*Illustrated London News*, Jan. 13, 1912; "The Romance of Orthodoxy," *Orthodoxy*; "A Defence of Bores," *Lunacy and Letters*)

decadence: to be wrong, and to be carefully wrong. ("The Nameless Man," *A Miscellany of Men*)

deconstruction: the ability to see everything about a story except the point. (*Land and Water*, Christmas 1917)

decorum: the morality of immoral societies. ("Conventions and the Hero," *Lunacy and Letters*)

degeneracy: going from bad to worse. (*Illustrated London News*, Mar. 15, 1913)

demagogue: the man who has little to say and says it loud. ("The Philosopher," *George Bernard Shaw*)

democracy: the million masks of god; direct government by

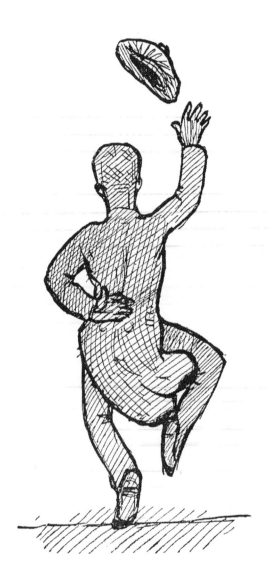

DANCING

DANGER

the people; a strange sort of place, where politics could be conducted even without politicians; the crowd ruling itself, like a king; the faith that the most terribly important things must be left to ordinary men themselves—the mating of the sexes, the rearing of the young, the laws of the state. ("Gold Leaves," *Collected Poems*; "The Case for Main Street" *Sidelights*; *Illustrated London News*, Nov. 17, 1923; "Very Christian Democracy," *Christendom in Dublin*; "The Ethics of Elfland," *Orthodoxy*)

desire: the wildest part of the soul. (*Daily News*, Oct. 13, 1906)

despotism: a tired democracy. As fatigue falls on a community, the citizens are less inclined for that eternal vigilance which has truly been called the price of liberty; and they prefer to arm only one single sentinel to watch the city while they sleep. ("The Antiquity of Civilization," *The Everlasting Man*)

detective story: a selected bundle of clues, with a few blinds as carefully selected as the clues. ("Public and Private Life," *Chaucer*)

Determinism: the absence of determination, the theory that no god, angel, animal or vegetable ever determined to do anything; the practical religion of cowards. ("Second Thoughts on Shaw," *George Bernard Shaw*; *Daily News*, Nov. 21, 1903)

Determinist: a morbid logician who makes the theory of causation quite clear and then finds that he cannot say "if you please" to the housemaid. ("The Maniac," *Orthodoxy*)

Diabolist: someone with such a hatred of heaven and earth that he has tried to take refuge in hell. ("The Escape from Paganism," *The Everlasting Man*)

DIABOLIST

diabolism: taking horror seriously. ("Hamlet and the Danes," *The Crimes of England*)

dignity: the expression of sacred personality and privacy. ("The Pedant and the Savage," *What's Wrong with the World*)

dirt: matter in the wrong place. (*New Witness*, Jan. 31, 1919)

disappointment: the dark surprise of youth. ("The Tragedy of the Patriot," *William Cobbett*)

disillusionment: a dark cloud of numbing illusion. (*Daily News*, Mar. 7, 1901)

distraction: psychological crucifixion. Though we talk of lightly of doing this or that to distract the mind, it remains really as well as verbally true that to be distracted is to be distraught. The original Latin word does not mean relaxation; it means being torn asunder as by wild horses. The original Greek word, which corresponds to it, is used in the text which says that Judas burst asunder in the midst. (*Illustrated London News*, Apr. 22, 1933)

Distributism: the theory that private property is proper to every private citizen; the right and essential thing that as many people as possible should have the natural, original forms of sustenance as their own property. (Introduction to Cecil Chesterton's *History of the United States*; *G.K.'s Weekly*, Sept. 17, 1932.)

divorce: the attempt to give respectability to a broken vow. (Pt. 7, *The Superstition of Divorce*)

doctrine: something that is taught; a definite point; immortal and unalterable truth. ("The New Hypocrite," *Illustrated London News*, Jan. 5, 1907; *What's Wrong with the World*; *Illustrated London News*, Mar. 23, 1929)

dog: a sort of curly tail to a man. (*Illustrated London News*, July 16, 1910)

dogma: a general term for any primary philosophical principle promulgated by the authority of somebody; anything of which a man might be certain but which other men might violently dispute; the serious satisfaction of the mind; the only thing that makes argument or reasoning possible. (*Daily News*, April 14, 1906; *Manchester Guardian*, Oct. 3, 1904; "American Notes," *Appreciations*; "The Victorian Compromise," *The Victorian Age in Literature*)

domesticity: a necessary social work being done for love when it cannot be done for money; and (one might almost dare to hint) presumably to be repaid with love since it is never repaid in money. ("The Drift from Domesticity," *The Thing*)

Doom: the oldest of all the Demons, who has always blighted mankind with superstitions of the destiny and death of races. (*Illustrated London News*, Feb. 15, 1930)

doubt: a weak and undeveloped condition; timid and indefinite destruction. (*Illustrated London News*, Jan. 31, 1931)

dragon: the most cosmopolitan of impossibilities. (*Illustrated London News*, Sept. 18, 1926)

dreams: prodigious landscapes, sensational incidents, and the fragments of half-decipherable stories shown to us without our choice in the sudden and astonishing trance we call sleep. ("The Meaning of Dreams," *Lunacy and Letters*)

drunk: being dazed with too much of a good thing. (*Daily News*, Sept. 25, 1909)

drunkard: the man who does not understand the delicate

DRUNKARD

and exquisite moment when he is moderately and reasonably drunk. ("On the Movies," *Generally Speaking*)

Dualism: the theory that good and evil are, in one sense at least, exactly balanced in the universe: that, in one sense at least, their balance creates the universe. The very pattern of the cosmos, so to speak, is a pattern of crossed swords. Life and death are fencing for ever; and the issue is always doubtful. (With a movement of iron self-control, I here refrain from making a pun about a Dualist and a duellist.) (*Illustrated London News*, May 31, 1913)

duel: a confession of equality; to settle quarrels by private war. (*Illustrated London News*, Aug. 8, 1914; *New York American*, April 2, 1932)

E

earnestness: German for "going about with your mouth open, ready to swallow anything, god or goblin, like so many flies." (*Illustrated London News*, June 15, 1912)

Earth: the new star we still have not found—the one on which we were born. ("A Defence of Baby Worship," *The Defendant*)

earthquake: a thing in which the largest thing we know begins to move, and to remind us for the first time of how long it has been lying still. (*Illustrated London News*, Dec. 16, 1916)

Easter: the spiritual New Year. (*Illustrated London News*, April 3, 1926)

eavesdropping: a conversation in which the listener is forbidden to join. (*G.K.'s Weekly*, May 3, 1930)

economics: the study of bread, which is more actual than

DUEL

EARTH

money, and not really the study of tables and statistics which are more remote than money. (*Illustrated London News*, Sept. 17, 1910)

economy: the management of a house; the realization of the value of everything. ("Tennyson," *A Handful of Authors*; "A Sermon on Cheapness," *The Apostle and the Wild Ducks*)

ecumenism: bridging the chasm between creeds by exalting the minority that is indifferent over the majority that is interested; trying to agree about nothing. ("The Shadow of the Problem," *The New Jerusalem*; *Daily News*, June 3, 1905)

editor: a journalist in authority, whose most familiar emotion is one of continuous fear; fear of libel actions, fear of lost advertisements, fear of misprints, fear of the sack. ("The Purple Wig," *The Wisdom of Father Brown*)

education: truth in a state of transmission; the soul of a society as it passes from one generation to the next; the teaching of anything to anybody. ("An Evil Cry," *What's Wrong with the World*; *Illustrated London News*, July 5, 1924; Jan. 26, 1907)

efficiency: doing something thoroughly, without thinking what it is; discovering everything about a machine except what it is for. (*New Witness*, Jan. 20, 1916; "Wanted: An Unpractical Man," *What's Wrong with the World*)

efficient: mechanical and calculated. A word that does not really tell us anything at all. Everything that has ever been done was, so far as it went, efficient, for efficient simply means contriving to get it done. ("The Idiot," *The Ball and the Cross*; *Daily News*, Oct. 14, 1905.)

egoist: a man making himself, and not something better than himself, the standard of everything. (*The Observer*, Nov. 30, 1919)

egomania: making the self the center of the universe (*Illustrated London News*, Dec. 2, 1933)

electioneering: organized lying. (*G.K.'s Weekly*, Dec. 26, 1935)

ellipsis: that string of little dots with which a writer often ends a sentence. It means "I could go on leaving off this subject forever." (*Daily News*, June 29, 1912)

emancipation: the free choice of the soul between one set of limitations and another. (*Daily News*, Dec. 21, 1905)

emotion: the irreducible minimum, the indestructible germ. (*Daily News*, Dec. 5, 1901)

empire: an authority from nowhere attempting to master an anarchy from everywhere. (*Illustrated London News*, Sept. 3, 1910)

employment: the exchange of one man's technical labor or talent for a fragment of another man's capital. (*Everyman*, Nov. 22, 1912)

enchantment: the fixed loss of oneself in some unnatural captivity or spiritual servitude. ("Hamlet and the Danes," *The Crimes of England*)

ennui: the great sin, the sin by which the whole universe tends continually to be undervalued and to vanish from the imagination. ("A Defence of Bores," *The Defendant*)

equality: the basis of all morality; the idea that every man should be reverenced like a king. (*Illustrated London News*, Jan. 20, 1906)

essay: the only literary form which confesses, in its very name, that the rash act known as writing is really a leap in the dark;

a short piece of prose without any narrative. ("The Essay," *Essays of the Year*, 1931; "Dombey and Son," *Appreciations*)

ethicist: a really reverent person who still insists on kneeling even when he has nothing to kneel to. (*Illustrated London News*, Feb. 24, 1912)

ethics: the science of conduct; the idea of morality founded solely upon science; decency for decency's sake, decency unborn of cosmic energies and barren of artistic flower. (*Illustrated London News*, June 12, 1909; *Daily News*, Jan. 9, 1904; "The Universal Stick," *What's Wrong with the World*)

Eugenics: a principle whereby the deepest things of the flesh and spirit must have the most direct relation with the dictatorship of the State; a denial of the Declaration of Independence. It urges that so far from all men being born equal, numbers of them ought not to be born at all. ("The Meanness of the Motive," *Eugenics and Other Evils*; *Illustrated London News*, Nov. 20, 1915)

euphemism: a refusal of people to say what they mean. (*Illustrated London News*, June 30, 1928)

Euthanasia: at present only a proposal for killing those who are a nuisance to themselves; but soon to be applied progressively to those who are a nuisance to other people. (*The American Review*, Feb. 1937)

evolution: a notion that things do themselves; the vision of all things coming from an egg, a dim and monstrous oval germ that laid itself by accident; the semi-scientific theory which expects every man to be as weak and vile as his heredity makes him. ("Hamlet and the Danes," *The Crimes of England*; "Wanted, An Unpractical Man," *What's Wrong with the World*; *Daily News*, Oct. 28, 1905)

exaggeration: the logical extension of something that really does exist; the transition from life to art. ("Charles Dickens: His Life," *Encyclopedia Britannica*, 1929; "The Enchanted Man," *A Miscellany of Men*)

exclusive: in commerce, a thing which pays not by attracting people but by turning people away. ("The Queer Feet," *The Innocence of Father Brown*)

executioner: somebody who does something—we do not want to think what. (*New Witness*, Jan. 20, 1916)

existence: the abyss of actuality, the fundamental fact of being; a stranger, and as a stranger I give it welcome; an enjoyment, when it can be uninterruptedly enjoyed, and this fact is never so vivid as just after the toothache has stopped. ("The Greatness of Chaucer," *Chaucer*; "The God with the Golden Key," *Autobiography*; *Illustrated London News*, Oct. 28, 1922)

Existentialism: a sense of poetical injustice. (*Illustrated London News*, Sept. 9, 1916)

experience: education when it is too true to be taught. (*G.K.'s Weekly*, April 25, 1935)

expert: a very opinionated person. (*Vital Speeches*, July 1, 1935)

F

fact: a thing which can be admitted without being explained. ("The Heroic that Happened," *Lunacy and Letters*)

fad: the setting up of the mood against the mind; a dislocation of the conditions of civilization in a degree disproportionate to the amelioration alleged (Now, let no one say that I cannot use long words, just as though I were a horny-headed Bolshevistic proletarian). (*William Blake*; *New York American*, Feb. 13, 1921)

EXECUTIONER

fairy tales: the uncommon things as seen by the common people. ("The Pickwick Papers," *Charles Dickens*)

Fairyland: a place of positive realities, plain laws, and a decisive story. (*Illustrated London News*, June 10, 1911)

faith: that which is able to survive a mood; believing the incredible; a certainty about something we cannot prove; divine frivolity. ("The Orthodoxy of Hamlet," *Lunacy and Letters*; "Paganism and Mr. Lowes Dickinson," *Heretics*; "Robert Louis Stevenson," *A Handful of Authors*)

Fall, The: A view of life that holds that we have misused a good world and not merely been entrapped into a bad one. ("The Outline of the Fall," *The Thing*)

fame: the old human glory, the applause and wonder of the people. ("Later Life and Works," *Charles Dickens*)

family: the thing on which all civilization is built; the idea that a man and a woman should live largely for the next generation and that they should, to some extent, defer their personal amusements, such as divorce and dissipation, for the benefit of the next generation. (*Illustrated London News*, Apr. 22, 1911; May 31, 1930)

fanatic: a man whose sense of a particular truth is too strong for his sense of the universal truth, even in so far as the larger truth supports the smaller; a man whose faith in something he thinks true makes him forget his general love of truth, and sometimes makes him forget the truth of that truth. (*Illustrated London News*, Mar. 7, 1925)

fanaticism: a fixed, but isolated and unfamiliar philosophy; mad along one idea. (*Daily News*, June 9, 1906; "The Paradoxes of Christianity," *Orthodoxy*)

fantastic: an acute artistic device for reviving in adults the pleasure which infancy has in the daily comedy of things. (*Daily News*, Sept. 9, 1911)

farce: theatrical art that appeals to the sense of humor in a highly simplified state. ("The Time of Transition," *Charles Dickens*)

fashion: the imitation of luxury and the leadership of wealth; a custom to which men cannot get accustomed; an ideal that fails to satisfy. (*G.K.'s Weekly*, July 13, 1929; "The Family and the Feud," *Irish Impressions*; *Illustrated London News*, July 2, 1921)

fashionable: anything on the brink of being old-fashioned. (*Illustrated London News*, Aug. 28, 1926)

fast: an exercise in the art of realization by absence. (*Illustrated London News*, Sept. 9, 1911)

father: a word still in use among the more ignorant and ill-paid of the industrial community; the badge of an old convention or unit called the family. A man and woman having vowed to be faithful to each other, the man makes himself responsible for all the children of the woman, and is thus generically called "Father." Father and the family are the foundations of thought. ("The End of the Household Gods," *Eugenics and Other Evils*)

fear: the belief that might is right. (*Daily News*, Feb. 17, 1906)

Feminism: the refusal to be feminine; a silly antagonism to man which manifests itself in a desire to abandon most of the habits of women; the plodding, elaborate, elephantine imitation of the male sex. (*Illustrated London News*, Aug.18, 1928;

FARCE

FASHION

G.K.'s Weekly, Dec. 26, 1925; "Folly and Female Education," *What's Wrong with the World*)

Feminist: one who dislikes the chief feminine characteristics. ("The Modern Slave," *What's Wrong with the World*)

fiction: the common things as seen by the uncommon people; a diary of day-dreams instead of days. ("The Pickwick Papers," *Charles Dickens*; *Illustrated London News*, Apr. 21, 1923)

fighting spirit: an interest in the enemy's movements in order to parry or to pierce them. (*Daily News*, Dec. 12, 1908)

Finishing School: a mysterious institution for finishing an education without ever beginning it. ("On Love," *All I Survey*)

fire: the most startling of all material things, a thing known only to man, the expression of his sublime externalism. It embodies all that is human in his hearths and all that is divine on his altars. It is the most human thing in the world, the purple and golden flag of the sons of Eve. But there is about this generous and rejoicing thing an alien and awful quality: the quality of torture. Its presence is life; its touch is death. Fire is the essence of nearly all ritual. To burn something, to make a blaze, is one of the most natural outcomes of strong conviction of any sort. ("The Man Who Thinks Backwards," *A Miscellany of Men*; *Illustrated London News*, Nov. 25, 1905)

first principle: the thing with which thought has to start, since it must start with something; the thing which cannot or need not be proved, either because it is self-evident or accepted by all parties. (*America*, June 6, 1926)

flattery: something that is at once a compliment and a lie. (*Illustrated London News*, May 4, 1918)

flippancy: the blackest of all the enemies of joy. (*Daily News*, May 21, 1901)

food: a primary necessity that can only be got from the earth; the most real of facts, the most unreal of issues. (*G.K.'s Weekly*, July 9, 1932; June 14, 1930)

fossil: the *form* of an animal or organism, from which all its own animal or organic substance has entirely disappeared; but which has kept its shape, because it has been filled up by some totally different substance by some process of distillation or secretion, so that we might almost say, as in the medieval metaphysics, that its substance has vanished and only its accidents remain. ("The Religion of the Fossils," *The Well and the Shallows*)

fountain: a paradox designed to show that water can flow upwards or flow uphill. ("The Outline of Sanity," *The Resurrection of Rome*)

free: responsible. (*G.K.'s Weekly*, July 17, 1926)

free love: free lust. ("Obstinate Orthodoxy," *The Thing*)

free speech: the theory that a truth is much larger and stranger and more many-sided than we know of, and that it is very much better at all costs to hear every one's account of it. ("Browning in Later Life," *Robert Browning*)

free thinker: a man who is not allowed to believe that miracles happen. (*Illustrated London News*, Nov. 14, 1908)

free thought: free thoughtlessness; thoughtless thought; persecuting all those who choose to think that Catholicism is true. ("The World Inside Out," *Catholic Church and Conversion*; "Ibsen," *A Handful of Authors*; "Return of the Romans," *The Resurrection of Rome*)

free will: the thrill of choice, which includes the tragic possibility of making the wrong choice. To be certain of free will is to be uncertain of success. ("The Sequel to St. Thomas," *St. Thomas Aquinas*; "American Notes," *Appreciations*)

free woman: generally, a married woman. ("The Great Victorian Novelists," *Victorian Age in Literature*)

freedom: the first of those great hungers by which a man realizes he does not live by bread alone; the part of man that in all myths and mysteries has put man highest above nature and nearest to the divine; fullness, especially fullness of life; a state in which we cannot oppress each other but still insult each other. ((*Illustrated London News*, April 20, 1912; *Daily News*, Sept. 7, 1912; "The Slavery of Free Verse," *Fancies vs. Fads*; *Illustrated London News*, Mar. 17, 1906)

friendship: an agreement under all the arguments; a relationship which is as splendid as love, and which, unlike love, is free; and yet which is somehow strangely sad, because, unlike love, it is without fruit. ("Dedication," *What's Wrong with the World*; *Daily News*, Oct. 31, 1906)

frivolity: a lack of the grasp of the fullness and value of things. ("The Frivolous Man," *The Common Man*)

fun: something more godlike even than humor. ("Shakespeare and the Germans," *The Blinded Soldiers and Sailors Gift Book*)

funeral: a festival of sorrow. (*Illustrated London News*, Dec. 5, 1925)

Futurism: If you ask me what Futurism is, I cannot tell you; even the Futurists themselves seem a little doubtful; perhaps they are waiting for the future to find out. ("The Futurists," *Alarms and Discursions*)

G

gambling: the vanity of guessing; the true delirium of doubt. ("The Oracle of the Dog," *Illustrated London News*, Oct. 12, 1912)

game: a concentrated form of recreation. ("The Man with the Golden Key," *Autobiography*)

garden: a beautiful thing, in a way that is completely natural because it is completely artificial. ("Christmas Books," *Appreciations*; "The Meaning of the Crusades," *The New Jerusalem*)

General Election: believed by antiquaries to be the remains of some system of self-government, it consists solely in asking the citizen such queries as, "Detect some difference between the two persons in frock coats placed before you at this election." ("The Thing," *A Miscellany of Men*)

generalization: a thing with which many people agree besides myself. (*Daily News*, Feb. 12, 1910)

geniality: strength to spare. ("On the Wit of Whistler," *Heretics*)

gentleman: a man with a particular kind of good manners produced by a particular kind of economic security and uninterrupted lineage, who obeys strange statutes, not to be found in any moral text-book, and practices strange virtues nameless from the beginning of the world; a man of a limpid kindliness, of an obvious and dignified humility, of a softness for noble memories and a readiness for any minute self-sacrifice. (*Daily*

GENTLEMAN

News, Nov. 6, 1909; "Charles II," *Varied Types*; *The Bookman*, April 1903)

ghost: a shadow of the resurrection. (*Illustrated London News*, May 30, 1936)

ghost story: that old and genial horror which nurses can hardly supply fast enough for the children who want it. (Introduction to *Appreciations*)

glory: an ambition that exists in men which is higher than greed and lower than religion. (*Illustrated London News*, Oct. 27, 1917)

God: the author and the authority of all things. ("The Other Side of the Desert," *The New Jerusalem*)

golf: an expensive way of playing marbles. (quoted in *The Portable Curmudgeon*)

goodness: the highest thing in the world. (*Daily News*, Feb. 27, 1904)

gossip: a continuous interest in all minor human matters, a refusal to "mind one's own business"—that heathen and egotistical commandment. (*Daily News*, Sept. 13, 1905)

Gothic Architecture: the mysticism that is in man made manifest in stone. (*Illustrated London News*, Feb. 23, 1924)

government: helping to rule the tribe; an accidental and even abnormal necessity, arising from the imperfection of life. ("The Ethics of Elfland," *Orthodoxy*; *New York American*, July 9, 1932)

gramophone: a machine for recording such tunes as certain shops and other organizations choose to sell. ("Babies and Distributism," *The Well and the Shallows*)

grass: a convenient metaphor for something always down-trodden and yet something never destroyed. (*Illustrated London News,* Aug. 3, 1935)

gratitude: happiness doubled by wonder. ("The Age of the Crusades," *A Short History of England*)

greatness: to be adored by antagonistic people for inconsistent reasons. (*Daily News*, Dec. 30, 1908)

greenhorn: the ultimate victor in everything because he is wise enough to be made a fool of. He makes himself comfortable in the traps that have been laid for him. He makes himself at home wherever he is "taken in." And because he is taken in everywhere he sees the inside of everything. ("The Pickwick Papers," *Charles Dickens*)

grotesque: the fierce and humorous energy in things, the defiant and wholesome ugliness of courage and experience. (*The Speaker*, Feb. 23, 1901)

grumbling: carelessness as applied to criticism; anger in solution. (*New Witness*, Feb. 17, 1916; *Illustrated London News*, May 24, 1919)

Grunky: a word which I invented at the age of five, to express my religious sentiments. (*Daily News*, May 14, 1904)

guild: a self-governing body trying to preserve the status of the profession. (*G.K.'s Weekly*, Dec. 19, 1925)

gusto: a boyish power of enjoyment. (*New York American*, Dec. 22, 1934)

H

habit: a thing a man could abandon and is not specially concerned with, but which he finds himself dropping into here and there in the varied concerns of life. (*Hearst's Magazine*, July, 1913)

happiness: a state of the soul in which our natures are full of the wine of an ancient youth, in which banquets last for ever, and roads lead everywhere, where all things are under the exuberant leadership of faith, hope, and charity. ("Charles Dickens," *The Bookmen*, May, 1903)

head: the thing that talks; an abnormal excrescence where, it has been conjectured, there dwells a principle called a Mind. (*Illustrated London News*, Apr. 22, 1911; Jan. 6, 1934)

health insurance: a stake men can only put down by being poorer than they are, and only get back by being sicker than they are. (*Illustrated London News*, Jan. 25, 1913)

Heaven: our native land. ("At Overroads Door," *Return to Chesterton*)

hedonism: being more sick of happiness than an invalid is sick of pain; an art sense that seeks the assistance of crime since it has exhausted nature. ("Savonarola," *Twelve Types*)

Hell: the place where nothing can happen; the home of dishonesty; the cosmic lunatic asylum; energy without joy; an infinity of falling. ("On the Alleged Optimism of Dickens," *Charles Dickens*; *Illustrated London News*, Nov. 28, 1909; *Daily News*, Nov. 23, 1907; Introduction to *Thackeray*; "Fear," *Lunacy and Letters*)

heraldry: a science of imagery. ("The Antiquity of Civilisation," *The Everlasting Man*)

heredity: that half-formed philosophy of fears and omens, of curses and weird recurrence and darkness and the doom of blood. ("The Unanswered Challenge," *Eugenics and Other Evils*)

HEAD

heresy: the exaltation of something which, even if true, is secondary or temporary in its nature against those things which are essential and eternal, those things which always prove themselves true in the long run; a truth taught out of proportion; a truth that hides all the other truths; an infectious disease of the intellect. (*William Blake*; *Daily News*, June 26, 1909; "St. Thomas More," *The Well and the Shallows*; "Ibsen," *A Handful of Authors*)

heretic: a man who prefers his criticism to his Catholicism; a man who loves his truth more than truth itself; a martyr to false gods. ("The Religion of Chaucer," *Chaucer*; "On Reading," *The Common Man*; *The Bookman*, April, 1903)

hero: a human who, by a certain godlike illogicality, is more human than humanity itself. (*Daily News*, April 30, 1904)

heroism: a blazing indiscretion. (*Illustrated London News*, May 27, 1911)

hill: a bulky feature in the landscape. (*Daily News*, April 4, 1908)

historian: one who has to explain the horrible mystery of how fashions were ever fashionable. (*Illustrated London News*, Oct. 8, 1910)

historians: the absent-minded race of men. (*Illustrated London News*, April 6, 1935)

history: a hill or high point of vantage from which men see the town in which they live or the age in which they are living. (*Illustrated London News*, June 18, 1932)

hobby: a sort of soothing madness. (*Daily News*, Feb. 11, 1905)

holiday: a holy day, a word that will always answer the ignorant slander which asserts that religion was opposed to human cheerfulness and will always assert that when a day is holy it should also be happy; a restoring thing that, by a blast of magic, turns man into himself. (*Illustrated London News*, Sep. 29, 1906; "The War on Holidays," *Utopia of Usurers*)

home: partly an inn for rest, partly a school for education, and partly a temple for the dedication of human souls to some unifying duties of life. (*Daily News*, Oct. 23, 1909)

hope: the thing that never deserts men and yet always, with daring diplomacy, threatens to desert them; hoping when things are hopeless; the power of being cheerful in circumstances which we know to be desperate. (*G. F. Watts*; "Paganism and Mr. Lowes Dickinson," *Heretics*)

horseracing: an activity that is so unexciting that people have been obliged to make an artificial arrangement whereby something shall happen to their balances at a bank before they can overcome their ingrained indifference to one horse or another. (*Daily News*, June 25, 1904)

hospitality: the most ancient of human virtues, the normal and dignified manner of mixing with the world; the way which leaves a certain responsibility, at once creative and vigilant, in the maker and master of the feast, and bids him, as in the parables and the nursery rhymes, to call in his neighbors to be his friends. (*Illustrated London News*, Mar. 12, 1927)

hostess: a woman whose talent is to make two people talk when they hate it, and part them when they are beginning to like it. ("When Doctors Agree," *The Paradoxes of Mr. Pond*)

housekeeping: the practice of a hundred arts and crafts. ("The End of Wisdom," *The Collected Works of G. K. Chesterton*, Vol. 14)

human: to be incalculable. (*Illustrated London News*, Feb. 9, 1907)

humanitarian: one who upholds the claims of all creatures against those of humanity. ("The Eternal Revolution," *Orthodoxy*)

humanitarianism: the horrible habit of helping human beings only through pitying them, and never through respecting them. ("About Voltaire," *As I Was Saying*)

Humanity: a thing most of us have never seen even in a vision. (*Daily News*, Feb. 11, 1905)

humility: the permanent human paradox that the best thing is something which a man may have, but which a man must not claim; the luxurious art of reducing ourselves to a point, not to a small thing or a large one, but to a thing with no size at all, so that to it all the cosmic things are what they really are—of immeasurable stature; a restraint upon the arrogance and infinity of the appetite of man; making the subjective objective—the realization that, to the universe, oneself is not I, but only he. (*Daily News*, July 28, 1906; "A Defence of Humility," *The Defendant*; "The Suicide of Thought," *Orthodoxy*; *Illustrated London News*, Feb. 26, 1916)

humor: a term which not only refuses to be defined, but in a sense boasts of being indefinable (and it would commonly be regarded as a deficiency in humor to search for a definition of humor); the most erratic of spiritual forces, eternally dancing between reason and unreason; the sentinel of humility; making game of man, that is, to dethrone him from his official dignity and hunt him like game; a subtle relish for the small incongruities of society. ("Humour," *The Spice of Life*; "The Library of the Nursery," *Lunacy and Letters*; *Illustrated*

HUMOR

London News, Nov. 4, 1916; "The Flat Freak," *Alarms and Discursions*; "Mark Twain," *A Handful of Authors*)

hygiene: the superstition of soap; the vision of humanity in a network of precautions against remote possibilities, so that a man must not drink from a well for want of a filter or keep a dog for fear of hydrophobia or let his little girl's hair grow for fear of verminous accidents. ("The School for Hypocrites," *What's Wrong with the World*; *Daily News*, Sept. 11, 1909)

hypocrisy: moral sentiments used for immoral objects. ("Rhymes for Children," *GKC as MC*)

hypocrite: the unluckiest of actors who is never out of a job. (*Illustrated London News*, June 13, 1914)

hypothesis: the unknown. ("The Empire of the Insect," *What's Wrong with the World*)

I

iconoclast: the lowest of all the unskilled trades. (*Daily News*, April 26, 1905)

idea: something that a man can agree or disagree with. (*Illustrated London News*, Aug. 9, 1930)

ideal: an aim; for many modern idealists, a thing that is only called an Ideal because it does not exist. It is at best a possibility, or perhaps only a pattern or abstract method of measurement. The less it is a Reality, the more it is an Ideal. (*Illustrated London News*, Jan. 28, 1933)

idealism: considering everything in its practical essence. ("An Unpractical Man," *What's Wrong with the World*)

idealist: a visionary; a man who believes more than he sees;

certainly a man who believes much more than other men believe. (*Illustrated London News*, April 7, 1934)

idol: the thing which wild human creatures (and tame human creatures too) make from some dark impulse to realize their own bad dreams. (*Illustrated London News*, Nov. 25, 1905)

idolatry: a condition that exists where the thing which originally gave us happiness becomes at last more important than happiness itself; the preference for the incidental good over the eternal good which it symbolizes; the elementary mathematical and moral heresy that the part is greater than the whole. ("Lunacy and Letters," *Lunacy and Letters*)

idiom: a language that has produced out of its own national history certain typical turns of phraseology that correspond to philosophy. (*New York American*, Aug. 10, 1935)

imagination: the mightiest of the pleasures; a thing of clear images. The more a thing becomes vague the less imaginative it is, the more a thing becomes wild and lawless the less imaginative it is. The function of imagination is not to make strange things settled, so much as to make settled things strange; not so much to make wonders facts as to make facts wonders. ("The Suicide of Thought," *Orthodoxy*; *Illustrated London News*, Mar. 24, 1906; "A Defence of China Shepherdesses," *The Defendant*)

immoralize: to moralize against morality. ("On Bright Old Things," *Sidelights*)

impartiality: a pompous name for indifference; another name for impossibility. (*The Speaker*, Dec. 15, 1900; *Illustrated London News*, Nov. 11, 1922)

Imperialism: the desire to possess distances even without enjoying them. (*Daily News*, Sept. 17, 1901)

Impressionism: the substitution of atmosphere for shape, the sacrifice of form to tint, the cloudland of the mere colorist; believing one's immediate impressions at the expense of one's more permanent and positive generalizations; putting what one notices above what one knows; the monstrous heresy that seeing is believing; that final skepticism which can find no floor to the universe. (*William Blake*; "The Criminals Chase the Police," *The Man Who Was Thursday*)

impulse: something which need not be explained because it cannot be explained, an airy, instinctive, intangible, innocent kind of prejudice; a slight and fleeting feeling that could not be explained to a policeman, which perhaps the very appearance of a policeman out of the bushes might destroy. (*Illustrated London News*, Aug. 10, 1907)

incarnation: the inevitable result of love, which leads to the inevitable result of crucifixion. (*Illustrated London News*, Aug. 20, 1927)

inconvenience: an adventure wrongly considered. ("On Running After One's Hat," *All Things Considered*)

indifference: an elegant name for ignorance. (*The Speaker*, Dec. 15, 1900)

individualism: the instinct of escape; a communal mass of selfishness. (*American Magazine*, April 1931; *Illustrated London News*, Feb. 25, 1928)

Industrialism: the system run by a small class of Capitalists on a theory of competitive contract; another name for hell.

("The Break-Up of the Compromise," *Victorian Age in Literature*)

industry: labouring incessantly to make labour-saving machines. (*G.K.'s Weekly*, Mar. 2, 1929)

infanticide: murder at its worst; not only the brand of Cain but the brand of Herod. (*Illustrated London News*, June 3, 1922)

injustice: the denial of right. (*Illustrated London News*, Feb. 3, 1917)

insomnia: one of the things which wealth cannot prevent, and education may possibly even promote. (*New Witness*, Aug. 29, 1919)

inspired: breathing from a bigger self and telling more than one knows. ("The Dramatist," *George Bernard Shaw*)

instinct: buried reason. (*Illustrated London News*, Jan. 22, 1916)

intellectuals: imbeciles whose minds have been mashed into mire by passing wagons of polysyllables, and have just breath enough left to say "reactionary," marked by the loose use of labels, the refusal to follow an argument; the scatter-brained pursuit of mere associations, and the total inability to write sense, but even to read it. (*New Witness*, Feb. 24, 1916)

intelligence: the power of dogmatizing rightly. (*Platitudes Undone*.)

irreligious: to doubt things which men's normal imagination does not necessarily doubt. ("The Break-up of the Compromise," *Victorian Age in Literature*)

INSOMNIA

J

Jazz: a nightmare of noise, recalling the horns of hell, generally accompanied by an undercurrent of battering monotony; the Song of the Treadmill. ("On the Prison of Jazz," *Avowals and Denials*)

Jingoism: irresponsibility, hysterical cruelty, looseness, vulgarity, and verbosity; in politics and patriotism, the habit of employing anger as a frivolity, drawing upon a reserve of wrath for a daily pleasure. (*Daily News*, June 26, 1901; May 25, 1907)

joke: something that need have no sense, except that one wild and supernatural sense which we call the sense of humor. ("The Flat Freak," *Alarms and Discursions*)

journalism: writing badly; writing badly on an enormous scale; the art of doing dull things in a hurry; a machine for multiplying and magnifying one small thing indefinitely; the art of pretending to know. ("On Writing Badly," *A Handful of Authors*; *Illustrated London News*, Feb. 7, 1925; *G.K.'s Weekly*, Mar. 28, 1925; Speech to the Johnson Society of London)

journalist: one who is vastly ignorant about many things, but who writes and talks about them all; a person who understands nothing except how to write about everything he does not understand. (*The New York Times*, Jan. 11, 1921; *Week-end Review*, Dec. 20, 1930)

joy: an elusive and elvish matter that is our reason for existing; the uproarious labor by which all things live. ("A Defence of Farce," *The Defendant*; "Authority and the Adventurer," *Orthodoxy*)

junk: treasures, of which the most precious are difficult to connect with any purpose whatever. ("The Mask of Midas," *The Collected Works of G. K. Chesterton*, Vol. 13)

jury: the only really representative parliament, because people do not want to serve on it. (*G.K.'s Weekly*, Nov. 11, 1932)

justice: the first human sense, which is the critic of all human institutions; an abstract, virgin, and wholly virtuous intolerance of a tale ending wrong; the refusal of the intellect to accept the prospect of everything being for ever upside down; a thing for which fools look in history and wise men in the Day of Judgment. (*Illustrated London News*, Aug. 17, 1907; Feb. 3, 1917; "Thomas Carlyle," *Varied Types*)

K

knife: a short sword. ("What I Found in My Pocket," *Tremendous Trifles*)

knighthood: originally, a title given to a man to further spur him to honor and bravery and chivalry. The knighthood in our time is not as a rule given to a man before, but rather after he is fortunate. The whole point of knighthood was that the knight should arrive late but not too late. Had St. George not been late there would have been no story. Had he been too late, there would have been no princess. (*Illustrated London News*, June 22, 1907; "The Eve of the War," *Gilbert Keith Chesterton*)

L

labor: the servant of exchange. (*G.K.'s Weekly*, Jan. 14, 1933)

language: an arbitrary system of grunts and squeals. (*G. F. Watts*)

Latitudinarian: the New Theologian of today who holds a high seat in that modern Parliament of Religions where all

KNIGHTHOOD

believers respect each other's unbelief. ("The New Theologian," *A Miscellany of Men*)

laughter: the power of uproarious reaction against ourselves and our own incongruities; the juncture of love and knowledge. (*Illustrated London News*, Sept. 9, 1922; Early Notebooks)

law: a thing that can be broken. ("A Fairy Tale," *Lunacy and Letters*)

learning: misled by the label on the bottle. ("The Victorian Compromise," *Victorian Age in Literature*)

legend: something that grows slowly and naturally and generally does symbolize some sort of relative truth about history; things that may never have happened, or, as some say, could never have happened, that are nevertheless rooted in our racial memory like things that have happened to ourselves; a thing that men vaguely cling to because it is true. ("The Tribal Triumph," *The End of the Armistice*; "The Romance of Rhyme," *Fancies vs. Fads*; *Illustrated London News*, Sept. 4, 1909)

leisure: a word that means three totally different things: 1. being allowed to do something, 2. being allowed to do anything, 3. being allowed to do nothing. (*Illustrated London News*, July 23, 1927)

Leisure State: the suggestion that mankind need not work, on the assumption that machinery will work. (*G.K.'s Weekly*, April 25, 1935)

Liberal: (n.) a man who, if he could by waving his hand in a dark room, stop all the deceivers of mankind forever, would not wave his hand. ("Browning in Italy," *Robert Browning*)

liberal: (adj.) a hospitality of the intellect and a hospitality of the heart. (Elizabeth Barrett Browning," *The Common Man*)

Liberalism: a hunger for humanity. (*Daily News*, Feb. 8, 1902)

Libertarianism: the unreasonable neglect of government. ("The Higher Anarchy," *What's Wrong with the World*)

liberty: the possession by a person of a certain limited imperium or circle of power within which he acts by choice and is a creator or an artist; the more mystical form of the true idea of property; the power of a thing to be itself; the living influence of the citizen on the State in the direction of molding or deflecting it; the very last idea that seems to occur to anybody, in considering any political or social proposal. (*New Witness*, July 27, 1916; July 23, 1920; "The Yellow Bird," *The Poet and the Lunatics*; "The Free Man," *A Miscellany of Men*; *Illustrated London News*, June 5, 1920)

life: a gift of God immensely valuable and immensely valued. ("Obstinate Orthodoxy," *The Thing*)

lion: a large, hairy sort of cat that happens to be living (or rather happens to be dying) in useless deserts that we have never seen and never want to see; a creature that never did us any good, and, in our circumstances, cannot even do us any harm; an overgrown stray cat. (*Illustrated London News*, Nov. 11, 1905)

literature: that rare sort of fiction which rises to a certain standard of objective beauty and truth; the record of the mysterious part of man that deals with that uncharted borderland of things where for so many thousand years the police of science and civilization have been outwitted by that outlaw, the soul. The aim of literature is to give something pointed in the mere form which shall correspond to something pointed, something inexpressibly pointed in the emotions. ("Fiction as Food I," *The Spice of Life*; *Daily News*, Oct. 10, 1901; May 12, 1906)

literary criticism: a string of labels. ("The History of a Half Truth," *Where All Roads Lead*)

locality: another name for liberty. ("Friends, Romans, Countrymen," *GKC as MC*)

logic: the fidelity and accuracy with which a certain process is performed, a process which can be performed with any materials, with any assumptions; sustained consistency of the mind; a machine of the mind; an intellectual sense of honor. (*Daily News*, Feb. 25, 1905; "Thomas Carlyle," *Varied Types*; *New Witness*, Aug. 4, 1922)

logomachy: the trick of taking a vague word and then asking if it applies precisely; using the same word in two senses and on both sides, as in the dreary old trick of comparing the enlightened condition of Buddhists with the benighted condition of Christians, by setting Christianity against itself, e.g., "Buddhism is Christianity, and Buddhism is better than Christianity, and Christianity will never be itself until it is enlightened enough to become something different." ((Introduction to *Thackeray*; *Illustrated London News*, Mar. 2, 1929)

love: the loneliness of God; a higher feeling than mere affectional convenience. It is a vision. It is heroic, and even saintly, in this: that it asks for nothing in return. ("Dr. Johnson," *GKC as MC*; "The Elf of Japan," *A Miscellany of Men*)

loyalty: the thing which operates where an obligation is felt to be unlimited; loving something as one loves one's mother, with an infinite gratitude for an infinite gift. ("Nationality and the French Wars," *A Short History of England*; *Illustrated London News*, Nov. 11, 1911)

lunatic: the man who lives in a small world but thinks it is a large one; the man who lives in a tenth of the truth, and thinks it is the whole. ("Dickens and America," *Charles Dickens*)

luxury: the pouring of the whole soul of passionately conscious art especially into unnecessary things; the only reward of the toils and crimes of the rich. ("The Rebellion of the Rich," *A Short History of England*; "Charles Dickens," *The Bookman*, 1903)

M

madman: not the man who has lost his reason, but the man who has lost everything except his reason. ("The Suicide of Thought," *Orthodoxy*)

madness: using mental activity so as to reach mental helplessness; that forest of deception and egotistical darkness. ("The Suicide of Thought," *Orthodoxy*; "A Museum of Souls," *The Ball and the Cross*)

magazine: a book of advertisements interleaved with literature; a thing one opens anywhere but at the beginning. Everybody reads a magazine, but nobody I ever heard of reads the first page of a magazine. (*New York American,* Sept. 26, 1931; *Illustrated London News*, May 21, 1910)

magic: 1.the abuse of preternatural powers, by lower agents whose work is preternatural but not supernatural; a monkey trick of imitation of the divine functions. 2. marvellousness. ("Magic and Fantasy in Fiction," *Sidelights*; "Browning in Later Life," *Robert Browning*)

MADNESS

man: a creature capable of reason and repentance; a beast whose superiority to other beasts consists in having fallen; a slightly disreputable animal who has been cast out from the community of beasts and birds perhaps because he does not share their innocence; an animal that makes dogmas; the only naked animal; a statue of God walking about the garden. (*Daily News*, Nov. 23, 1907; "A Discussion Somewhat in the Air," *The Ball And The Cross*; *Daily News*, July 2, 1910; "Concluding Remarks," *Heretics*; "The Man Who Thinks Backwards," *A Miscellany of Men*; "The Paradoxes of Christianity," *Orthodoxy*)

Manichee: one who believed that physical nature was made by the Devil, but was rescued by a pure Spirit; one of the many heresies which held sexuality blameless if it brought forth no offspring. (*T.P.'s Weekly*, July 4, 1914)

manners: those grand rhythms of the social harmony. ("Dickens and America," *Charles Dickens*)

marriage: the ancient bridge built between the two towers of sex; the only voluntary state on earth; the only state which creates and which loves its citizens; a duel to the death which no man of honor should decline. ("Superstition of Divorce-2," *Superstition of Divorce*; "Marriage and the Modern Mind," *Sidelights*; "The Wild Weddings," *Manalive*)

martyr: a man who cares so much for something outside him, that he forgets his own personal life. ("The Flag of the World," *Orthodoxy*)

Marxism: The theory that all the important things in history are rooted in an economic motive, that history is a science, a science of the search for food. (*Daily News*, July 31, 1909)

masterpiece: a thing that matters; art that we cannot expect even when we have seen it. (*Illustrated London News*, Aug. 17, 1924; *Century Magazine*, Dec., 1922)

Materialism: a faith in a fixed and godless fate; a deep and sincere faith in the incurable routine of the cosmos; a dingy, nineteenth-century fad, puffed into fashion by that preposterous old Prussian humbug, Haeckel. It advocates a political liberty, but it denies spiritual liberty. That is, it abolishes the laws which could be broken, and substitutes laws that cannot. Possibly the narrowest of all human sects, since it has the fewest vistas and the fewest doubts. ("The Romance of Orthodoxy," *Orthodoxy*; *Illustrated London News*, Mar. 29, 1919; "Mr. McCabe . . . " *Heretics*; *Illustrated London News*, Dec. 22, 1906)

Materialist: one whose mind is made of a kind of hardened mud; a man of simple faith, who believes that science is always right so long as it confines itself to proving that religions is wrong. (*Illustrated London News*, Jan. 20, 1912; May 9, 1931)

matriarchy: moral anarchy, in which the mother alone remains fixed because all the fathers are fugitive and irresponsible. ("Professors and Prehistoric Men," *The Everlasting Man*)

meaning: something that must have someone to mean it. ("The Ethics of Elfland," *Orthodoxy*)

megalomania: a love of living with one's inferiors. ("The Charm of Jingoism," *What's Wrong with the World*)

melancholy: a certain ghastly indolence of sorrow, an aching sterility in the hours, the sorrow of an endless afternoon. ("The Bones of a Poem," *A Handful of Authors*)

melodrama: theatrical art that appeals to the moral sense in a highly simplified state. ("The Time of Transition," *Charles Dickens*)

merry: the noble old English word that signifies that type of pleasure which excludes the pleasure of dignity. (*T.P.'s Weekly*, Christmas Number, 1914)

metaphor: a description that is at once vivid and vague. (*Illustrated London News*, June 1, 1918)

militarism: that sociological state when the engine employed to defend the society against hostile societies preponderates too much in the settlement of the society's internal affairs. (*Illustrated London News*, July 26, 1913)

miracle: power coming directly from God (or the devil) instead of indirectly through nature and human wills; an event that means Materialism is nonsense; a marvel, that is to say, a very rare and a very unexpected thing; fragmentary manifestations which must, even for their own purpose, be few and far between. (If it could be done by anybody at any minute, it could not fulfill the function, true or false, which its supporters suppose it to fulfill.); the liberty of God. ("The Wrong Shape," *The Innocence of Father Brown*; "An Example and a Question," *Irish Impressions*; *Illustrated London News*, Mar. 21, 1914; "The Romance of Orthodoxy," *Orthodoxy*)

mirror: a picture frame that holds hundreds of different pictures, all vivid and all vanished forever. ("The Mirror of the Magistrate," *The Secret of Father Brown*)

miser: a man who is intercepted and misled in his pursuit of thrift and betrayed into turning to the pursuit of money; the man who starves himself, and everybody else, in order to worship wealth in its dead form, as distinct from its living form. (*Illustrated London News*, June 29, 1935)

Missing Link: a runaway parent who is still dear to his family. He is not an animal, or even an argument, but simply the failure of an argument. He is a hole, a hiatus, a gap where a case breaks down. It is as if a man went climbing trees in a tropical forest looking for the fallacy of the undistributed middle. (*Illustrated London News*, Dec. 21, 1912; Nov. 13, 1920)

mob: the simplest element of humanity, because it is the deepest; the sub-consciousness of society. That is why it rises so rarely to the surface; and that is why, when it does rise, it is as awful as the unveiling of a god. (*Daily News*, Dec. 18, 1909)

Moderates: the political party with no policy; they wish streets to be Moderately passable, water to be Moderately drinkable, houses to be Moderately free from open drains, and politics to be Moderately free from open bribery. (*Daily News*, Feb. 9, 1907)

moderation: a deadlock of prejudices (*Illustrated London News*, Nov. 29, 1919)

Modern Age: The Muddle Ages. (*Illustrated London News*, Apr. 26, 1919)

Modern art: the antithesis of art; a shapeless lump of futility that does not please and does not even startle; utterly dreary disproportion, utterly commonplace irrelevancy, a disgusting nightmare that does not even frighten, but simply tires the mind with unmeaning sights and featureless landscapes and unmeaning words. (*Illustrated London News*, Mar. 24, 1906)

Modern literature: the echo of a silence. (*Illustrated London News*, July 31, 1926)

Modern martyr: a man chaining himself up and then complaining that he is not free. (*Illustrated London News*, Feb. 1, 1908)

Modern mind: a curious mixture of decayed Calvinism and diluted Buddhism; a door with no house to it. ("On the Novel without a Purpose," *The Thing*; "The Anarchist," *Alarms and Discursions*)

Modern philosophy: a philosophical resignation to its own helplessness. (*Illustrated London News*, July 31, 1926)

Modern thinker: a man who combines an expansive and exhaustive reason with a contracted common sense. ("The Maniac," *Orthodoxy*)

Modern thought: nothing. ("The Puritan," *George Bernard Shaw*)

Modern town: a place where there are no neighbors, but only strangers next door. (*Illustrated London News*, April 20, 1918)

Modernism: a form of snobbishness; a euphemism for muddle-headedness. ("The Case for the Ephemeral," *All Things Considered*; *G.K.'s Weekly*, May 10, 1930)

Modernist: one who mistakes experience for existence, and supposes that what he sees is all that there is to see. ("Changing Human Nature." *As I Was Saying*)

Modernity: the seeking for the truth in terms of time; the habit of dwelling disproportionately on the abnormal and the diseased. ("The Dramatist," *George Bernard Shaw*; *Illustrated London News*, June 25, 1910)

modernness: the abstract virtue of being alive at the present moment when we might all so easily have been dead one hundred or a thousand years ago. (*G.K.'s Weekly*, June 8, 1929)

modesty: the balance between mere pride and mere prostration. ("The Paradoxes of Christianity," *Orthodoxy*)

monism: the idea that all things are really only one thing. (Introduction to *Cosmology*)

monogamy: the one complete adventure of man. (*Daily News*, Oct. 28, 1905)

monomania: the state in which everything is neglected that one thing may be exaggerated. ("The Way of the Desert," *The New Jerusalem*)

monopoly: money without morals, which makes nonsense of the freedom we have gained. (*The Listener*, June 19, 1935)

moods: a raging and shifting series of frames of mind. ("The Seven Moods of Dorian," *The Flying Inn*)

moon: that timeless clock of all lunatics. (The Seven Moods of Dorian," *The Flying Inn*)

morality: the science of deeds. (*Illustrated London News*, Jan. 8, 1916)

morocracy: rule by the weak-minded. (*Illustrated London News*, April 13, 1912)

mother: a queen of life ("Folly and Female Education," *What's Wrong with the World*)

mother-in-law: a mystical blend of two inconsistent things— law and a mother. ("Wisdom and the Weather," *What's Wrong with the World*)

mountain: a stationary and reliable object which it is not necessary to chain up at night like a dog. ("A Defence of Rash Vows," *The Defendant*)

mud: the oldest and perhaps the mightiest of the enemies of man; a formless, featureless, colorless abomination; a corruption because it is a compromise: it is earth on which no man can walk; it is water in which no man can wash. (*New Witness*, Oct. 26, 1916; Jan. 31, 1919)

murder: private killing. (*G.K.'s Weekly*, April 5, 1934)

museum: a new conception, which, like so many modern conceptions, is based on a blunder in psychology and a blindness to the true interests of culture. It is meant for the mere slave of a routine of self-education to stuff himself with every sort of incongruous intellectual food in one indigestible meal. (*Illustrated London News*, Feb. 28, 1931)

mushrooms: the weird-hued and one-legged goblins of the forest. ("Vegetarianism in the Forest," *The Flying Inn*)

music: mere beauty, beauty in the abstract, beauty in solution. It is a shapeless and liquid element of beauty, in which a man may really float, not indeed affirming the truth, but not denying it. ("The Critic," *George Bernard Shaw*)

mustard: a condiment, a small luxury; a thing in its nature not to be taken in quantity; a pungent pleasure. ("The Broken Rainbow," *What's Wrong with the World*)

mystic: a man who finds a meaning in everything. ("Victor Hugo," *A Handful of Authors*)

mysticism: a sense of the mystery of things, the most gigantic form of common sense. (*Daily News*, Aug. 30, 1901)

myth: the gossip of the gods. ("Man and Mythologies," *The Everlasting Man*)

mythology: the ancient unfathomable wells which go down deeper than the reason into the very roots of the world, but contain the springs that refresh the reason and keep it active forever. The object of the rationalist historian is to choke up those wells. He puts in a sort of plug, like a stupid plumber, to stop the flowing of the fountain of youth. (*Illustrated London News*, Aug. 6, 1932)

N

narrowness: the negative side of simplicity and sincerity. (*Illustrated London News*, Oct. 28, 1922)

nasty: persons who fail to affect me with moral charm. (*Daily News*, Aug. 4, 1906)

nation: a society with a soul; a thing which recognizes a certain moral principle called patriotism, of which the opposite is treason. (*Everybody's Magazine*, Oct., 1914; *Illustrated London News*, May 14, 1912)

Nationalism: the idea that nations should respect *each other's* nationality. ("The Heresy of Race," *The End of the Armistice*)

nationality: another name for international misunderstanding. (*Illustrated London News*, June 7, 1924)

natural: consistent with the nature of things. (*Illustrated London News*, Mar. 29, 1919)

Natural Law: the right reason in things which man with his unaided reason can see to be right. (*American Review*, Sept., 1935)

Nature: what the wiser of us call Creation. (*G.K.'s Weekly*, Oct. 25, 1930)

neighbor: the most terrible of beasts, as strange as the stars, as reckless and indifferent as the rain. That is why the old religions and the old scriptural language showed so sharp a wisdom when they spoke, not of one's duty towards humanity, but one's duty towards one's neighbor. ("On Certain Modern Writers and the Institution of the Family," *Heretics*)

new: that which has no ascertained experience behind it. (*Illustrated London News*, Nov. 18, 1911)

newspaper: a loud and regular organ by which our civilization daily proclaims that it has nothing to say. ("The Moral of the Story," *Chaucer*)

newspaper press: a machine for destroying the public memory. (*G.K.'s Weekly*, Nov. 21, 1931)

nice: the weakest word ever used, or rather misused by man. ("The Slavery of Free Verse," *Fancies vs. Fads*)

nightmare: the horse that can ride on a man. (*Illustrated London News*, April 7, 1923)

nihilist: a revolutionist with nothing to revolt about. ("The Sceptic as Critic," *The Thing*)

non-partisan: impartial; undenominational; undogmatic; non-political; non-controversial; people who have never disputed their own dogma, and do not even know that it has ever been disputed; people who suppose the whole world to be of their denomination, and therefore anything that agrees with them is universal and anything that disagrees with them is insane. (*Illustrated London News*, Mar. 22, 1924)

nonsense: humor which has for the moment renounced all connection with wit; humor that abandons all attempt at intellectual justification, and does not merely jest at the incongruity of some accident or practical joke, as a by-product of real

NIGHTMARE

life, but extracts and enjoys it for its own sake; folly for folly's sake. ("Humour," *The Spice of Life*)

notion: an incomplete idea. (*New Witness*, Jan. 24, 1919)

novel: a fictitious narrative of which the essential is that the story is not told for the sake of the naked pointedness as an anecdote, or for the sake of the irrelevant landscapes and visions that can be caught up in it, but for the sake of some study of the difference between human beings. ("The Great Victorian Novelists," *Victorian Age*)

novelties: neglected antiquities. (*Illustrated London News*, Mar. 29, 1924)

Nudism: a fad connected with that particular sort of glorification of the body which generally goes with a certain weakness in the head. (*Illustrated London News*, Jan. 10, 1931)

nuisance: that by which one man doing as he likes burdens another with what he dislikes. (*New York American*, Sept. 24, 1932)

O

obedience: the most passionate form of personal choice. (*Daily News*, Dec. 13, 1901)

obscurantists: those who do not give information to the public when they could give it, and are supposed to be giving it, who do not want to show the truth, but only want to show that they possess it. (*Hearst's Magazine*, Dec., 1913)

octopus: half-a-dozen snakes with one head. (*Illustrated London News*, Oct. 21, 1911)

Oligarchy: a few men forming a governing group small

enough to be insolent and large enough to be irresponsible. ("Peace and the Papacy," *The Thing*)

opera: tragic and tremendous voices, shaking the heart and opening the depths of human nature like a day of judgment. ("The Holy Island," *The Resurrection of Rome*)

open-minded: insisting on the sameness of everything. (*Illustrated London News*, Jan. 6, 1923)

opinion: a general view that we have of existence, whether we like it or not, that alters everything we say or do, whether we like it or not, which may be more fantastic or more beautiful than we think, but which we will discover only if we are willing to search and dig for it. ("Concluding Remarks," *Heretics*)

optimism: a sort of cheap cheeriness, at the back of which there is a curious sort of hollow unbelief in reality; a mere worldly weakness of encouraging the world to do whatever it happens to be doing; an attempt to whitewash evil. (*Illustrated London News*, Aug. 30, 1930; *G.K.'s Weekly*, July 13, 1939; "On the Alleged Optimism of Dickens," *Charles Dickens*)

optimist: a person who thinks everything good except the pessimist. ("The Flag of the World," *Orthodoxy*)

ordeal: a test, something deliberately set up to try or prove a man especially touching his sincerity (but journalists use it as if it meant any kind of unpleasant experience, however much it be without purpose or without result). (*Illustrated London News*, Jan. 12, 1924)

ordinary: the acceptance of an order, a Creator and the Creation, the common sense of gratitude for Creation, life and love as gifts permanently good. ("Obstinate Orthodoxy," *The Thing*)

organization: turning men into machinery. (*Illustrated London News*, April 1, 1922)

originality: the power of returning to origins; disagreement with others; the power of going behind the common mind, discovering what it desires as distinct from what it says it desires, satisfying the sub-consciousness. (*Illustrated London News*, Sept. 20, 1919; "Concluding Remarks," *Heretics*; "Peter Pan as a Novel," *G.K. Chesterton Quarterly*, Autumn 2001)

Orthodoxy: that primary principle, or right reason in things, by which they can be judged independently of new fads or of old prejudices; an intrinsic intellectual rightness that can be judged in all times on its own terms; The Apostle's Creed. (*Illustrated London News*, July 6, 1935; "Introductory Remarks," *Orthodoxy*)

ownership: honor and independence. ("The Hobby and the Headwaiter," *The Apostle and the Wild Ducks*)

P

Pacifism: the contemptible repudiation of all loyalties; the wild promise not to fight for anything however just, in any position, however perilous, under any provocation, however abominable; proving that our enemies are so wicked that it must be safe to treat them as friends. (*G.K.'s Weekly*, Jan. 3, 1935; *Illustrated London News*, Apr. 5, 1924)

Pagan: a man who looks for his pleasures to the natural forces of this world, but who does not insist so strictly upon dry negations about the other. ("A Century of Emancipation," *The Well and the Shallows*)

Paganism: practical materialism without the narrowness of theoretical materialism. ("A Century of Emancipation," *The Well and the Shallows*)

Pantheism: the belief that the divine essence is equally distributed at any given moment in all the atoms of the universe. ("The Soul in Every Legend," *The Spice of Life*)

Pantheist: a person who is forced to pretend, in a priggish way, that all things are equally divine. ("The World Inside Out," *Catholic Church and Conversion*)

Papacy: the supreme tribunal of Christendom; the oldest, immeasurably the oldest, throne in Europe, and the only one that a peasant could climb. ("The Three Orders," *St. Francis of Assisi*; *Illustrated London News*, Aug. 29, 1914)

Paradise: purity and freedom. ("On Lying in Bed," *Tremendous Trifles*)

paradox: a statement that seems to contain a contradiction or to be intrinsically improbable; a statement that happens to be different from the catchwords common at a particular moment; an idea expressed in a form which is verbally contradictory; some kind of collision between what is seemingly and what is really true. (*Illustrated London News*, Aug. 1, 1925; "The Philosopher," *George Bernard Shaw*)

parents: those colossal benefactors of mankind. (*Daily News*, June 24, 1905)

Parliament: a frivolous debating club (*Illustrated London News*, Nov. 12, 1910)

parody: a superficial contrast covering a substantial congruity. ("The Pantomime," *The Common Man*)

partisan: a person acting from private friendship and personal conviction. (*New Witness,* Sept. 5, 1919)

patriotism: the normal and healthy affection of every man for his own nation; the real pride of real people in their town. (*Illustrated London News*, Apr. 18, 1931; Aug. 8, 1908)

peace: happiness, fulfillment and repose. (*Daily News*, Oct. 26, 1912)

peasant: the most permanently human of humanity; the man nearest to the realities of life; a man who manages to make his own field pay by his own labor. (*Illustrated London News*, Nov. 19, 1910; *Christian Science Monitor*, Mar. 22, 1912; *New Witness*, Jan. 21, 1921)

pedant: a person radically and incurably incompetent to grasp the real truth about anything. ("Italy and the German Professors," *The Book of Italy*)

pedantry: a pigmy practical joke, played by the half-educated on the uneducated. (*New Witness,* Dec. 9, 1915)

people: a hundred statues walking about the street, alive with the miracle of a mysterious vitality, a marvelous and impressive work of God. (*Illustrated London News*, Feb. 28, 1931)

permanence: ideas judged on their own merits without reference to the external modes of the age. (*Illustrated London News*, Mar. 5, 1927)

persecution: the imposition by the police of a widely disputed theory, incapable of final proof . ("The Established Church of Doubt," *Eugenics and Other Evils*)

perspective: the fancy that Nature keeps one's uncle in an

PEOPLE

infinite number of sizes, according to where he is to stand. ("The Triumph of the Donkey," *Alarms and Discursions*)

pessimism: a modern irritation, an itch to torment the spirit; a debased and barbarous superstition, a denial of all value in existence of any kind; a renunciation of the universe as well as the world; the belief in the failure of existence and the harmonious hostility of the stars. (*Illustrated London News*, Oct. 20, 1923; June 10, 1922; *G.K.'s Weekly*, June 13, 1929; "The Optimism of Byron," *Twelve Types*)

pessimist: a man who thinks everything is bad except himself, who thinks he is living in the worst of all possible worlds but is the best of all possible judges of it. ("The Flag of the World," *Orthodoxy*; "The Bones of a Poem," *A Handful of Authors*)

philanthropist: one who loves anthropoids; a benevolent bully. ("The Problem of St. Francis, *St. Francis of Assisi*; "Dickens and Christmas," *Charles Dickens*)

philanthropy: a version of charity which is a parody of charity; the cheap advice to live cheaply, the base advice to live basely, above all, the preposterous primary assumption that the rich are to advise the poor and not the poor the rich. ("Belfast and the Religious Problem," *Irish Impressions*; "Dickens and Christmas," *Charles Dickens*)

philistine: a man who is right without knowing why. ("The Song of the Flying Fish," *The Secret of Father Brown*)

philosophy: thought that has been thought out. ("The Revival of Philosophy," *The Common Man*)

picture: the attempt to stop the dissolving view from dissolving. (*Illustrated London News*, Feb. 14, 1925)

plain: uncommonly ugly. ("Dombey and Son," *Appreciations*)

plan: a combination of certain selected circumstances, and with all the chances against it except for those circumstances. (*New Witness*, Aug. 5, 1915)

plants: brutes tied with green rope. ("The Modern Manichee," *Collected Poems*)

platitudes: utterances that in certain circumstances are the only possible thing to say—because they are true. ("The Conscript and the Crisis," *A Miscellany of Men*)

play: doing what you like. ("Tommy and the Traditions," *Lunacy and Letters*)

pleasure: an ornament of life. ("The New Raid," *Utopia of Usurers*)

poet: a man who mixes up heaven and earth unconsciously, who makes men realize how great are the great emotions which they, in a smaller way, have already experienced. (*William Blake*; "The Greatness of Chaucer," *Chaucer*)

poetry: the algebra of life; that part of language made up of the echoes of words more than the words themselves; the imaginative reason when it rises almost to touch an imaginative unreason; emotions remembered in tranquility. ("Browning and his Ideal," *A Handful of Authors*; *Illustrated London News*, Jan. 8, 1927; Oct. 15, 1921; *New York American*, Aug. 20, 1935)

policeman: the representative and guardian of the city (*polis*), the symbol of human civilization; not merely a heavy man with a truncheon: a policeman is a machine for the smoothing and sweetening of the accidents of everyday existence.

In other words, a policeman is politeness: a veiled image of politeness—sometimes impenetrably veiled. (*Illustrated London News*, Sept. 29, 1906)

politeness: the atmosphere and ritual of the city (*polis*), the symbol of human civilization; not a thing merely suave and deprecating, but an armed guard, stern and splendid and vigilant, watching over all the ways of men; in other words, politeness is a policeman. (*Illustrated London News*, Sept. 29, 1906)

political liberty: the power of saying the sort of things that a decent but discontented citizen wants to say. ("The Free Man," *A Miscellany of Men*)

politician: a man who passes the first half of his life in explaining that he can do something, and the second half of it in explaining that he cannot; a man who persuades the people that they really want what he wants. (*Illustrated London News*, Mar. 30, 1918; Dec. 22, 1906)

politics: endless lobbying and more or less corrupt compromises; the survival of the fussiest. (*Illustrated London News*, Dec. 20, 1930; Dec. 16, 1905)

polytheism: the worship of gods who are not God ("The Other Side of the Desert," *The New Jerusalem*)

poor: the great mass of mankind. ("The Boyhood of Dickens," *Charles Dickens*)

popular prejudice: the bristly hide of a living principle. (*Illustrated London News*, May 13, 1911)

popular science: that which puts us to sleep to a lullaby of long words. ("A Real Danger," *Utopia of Usurers*)

popularity: giving the people what they want, a thing every inch as essential and idealistic in art as it is in politics. ("Peter Pan as a Novel," *G.K. Chesterton Quarterly*, Autumn 2001)

pornography: a system of deliberate erotic stimulants—not a thing to be argued about with one's intellect but to be stamped on with one's heel. ("Rabelaisian Regrets," *The Common Man*)

posterity: the most bankrupt of all debtors. ("The Library of the Nursery," *Lunacy and Letters*)

practical politician: a professional politician; a person of so firm a character and so rich an experience that nobody in the world can, by any wiles whatever, induce him to do anything at all. He never does anything. That is where his practicability comes in. ("A Summary," *The Outline of Sanity*; *Daily News*, Feb., 10, 1906)

practicality: a preference for prompt effort and energy over doubt and delay. ("Francis the Fighter," *St. Francis of Assisi*)

Pragmatism: the philosophical idea that the sun being useful is the same thing as the sun being there; a cosmic system made out of odds and ends. (*Illustrated London News*, Sept 17, 1910; "What Novelists Are For," *The Common Man*)

Pragmatist: one who sets out to be practical, but his practicality turns out to be entirely theoretical. ("The Approach To Thomism," *St. Thomas Aquinas*)

precious: something that is bought with a price, not merely a sumptuous thing, in the sense of something connected with gross luxury and wealth, but often in the sense of the ancient price of sacrifice. ("The Countrymen of Mary Webb and Thomas Hardy," *The Apostle and the Wild Ducks*)

prehistoric: unhistorical; before the beginning of our history;

the time before any connected narratives that we can read. ("The Defeat of the Barbarians," *A Short History of England*; *Illustrated London News*, May 9, 1925; "Professors and Prehistoric Men," *The Everlasting Man*)

prejudice: an unconscious dogma; an opinion held by somebody who has forgotten where it came from; something in your life for which you will hold meetings and agitate and write letters to the newspaper, but for which you will not find the plain terms of a creed. (*Illustrated London News*, Mar. 15, 1919; Introduction to *Letters on Polish Affairs*; "Rabelaisian Regrets," *The Common Man*)

pride: the falsification of fact by the introduction of self, the enduring blunder of mankind; the absolute annihilation which made devils and destroys men; that which cannot enjoy unless it controls; the ultimate human evil, the poison in every other vice. ("Christendom and Pride," *The End of the Armistice*; *The Observer*, Nov. 30, 1919; *Illustrated London News*, April 9, 1910; Aug. 22, 1914)

prig: one who has pride in the possession of his brain rather than joy in the use of it. (*Illustrated London News*, June 12, 1909)

prism: glass which shatters the daylight into colors and stains the white radiance of eternity. ("The True Victorian Hypocrisy," *Sidelights*)

profanity: the loss of holy fear. (*G.K.'s Weekly*, Mar. 8, 1934)

progress: going towards going on; a comparative of which we have not settled the superlative; the meaningless modern fancy of perpetually advancing into the white fog of a formless future, that everything has always perpetually gone right by accident; a sort of atheistic optimism, based on an ever-lasting coincidence far more miraculous than a miracle. Progress should mean that we are always changing the world to fit the vision. Progress does mean (just now) that we are always changing the vision. ("The Priest Of Spring," *A Miscellany of Men*; "On the Negative Spirit," *Heretics*; *Illustrated London News*, Dec. 20, 1913; "Wells and the World State," *What I Saw in America*; "The Eternal Revolution," *Orthodoxy*)

propaganda: believing that other people will believe whatever you invent. ("About Loving Germans," *As I Was Saying*)

property: appropriateness; the fact that something is *proper* to somebody; the positive form of liberty; the things that can be offered in courtesy, or expended in hospitality, or defended in honor; the art of democracy. (*Daily News*, Dec. 21, 1912; *Illustrated London News*, Nov. 14, 1908; Oct. 20, 1928; Oct. 25, 1919; "The Enemies of Property," *What's Wrong with the World*)

proportion: the principle of all reality. ("The Man in the Cave," *The Everlasting Man*)

prose: fragments of poetry; poetry interrupted. ("The Slavery of Free Verse," *Fancies vs. Fads*)

prostitution: selling what is sacred. ("The Beginning of the Quarrel," *The Outline of Sanity*)

provincial: one who suffers by being too much tied to one of the provinces of the old Roman civilisation, sometimes called Christendom, and too little in touch with the traditions of all the rest of it. (*G.K.'s Weekly*, Oct. 16, 1926)

Prussia: a bitter breeding ground of crude and cranky ideas. ("One Word More," *The End of the Armistice*)

psychoanalysis: a science conducted by lunatics for lunatics; confession without absolution. (*Illustrated London News*, June 23, 1928; "Fads and Public Opinion," *What I Saw in America*)

psychology: being off your chump. ("The Honour of Israel Gow," *The Innocence of Father Brown*)

public monument: the art of the open air. ("A Defence of Publicity," *The Defendant*)

publicity: the absence of criticism; the system that only allows us to know all the best that the rich choose to say about themselves; the public praise of a secret process; the enlargement of trade marks, but not the diminishment of trade secrets. (*G.K.'s Weekly*, Sept. 17, 1927; "The Return of the Romans," *The Resurrection of Rome*; *Illustrated London News*, Dec. 29, 1928)

publishing: making bad old books into worse new ones. ("A Much-Engaged Couple," *Return to Chesterton*)

punishment: a reaction and an expiation; the revolt of all men against the man who thinks he is the only man in the world. (*Daily News*, May 15, 1909)

Puritan: someone whose scruples are at once violent and trivial. Historically, the Puritan substituted a God who wished to damn people for a God who wished to save them. ("They are all Puritans," *Sidelights*)

Puritanism: righteous indignation about the wrong things; a version of purity which is a parody of purity; a paralysis which stiffens into Stoicism when it loses religion. ("They are all Puritans," *Sidelights*; "Belfast and the Religious Problem," *Irish Impressions*; "The Incomplete Traveller," *Autobiography*)

Q

quackery: false science. (*Illustrated London News*, July 12, 1930)

quarrel: a mutual appeal to conscience. (*Illustrated London News*, Jan. 8, 1916)

quiddity: the simplest and soundest human feeling about what a thing is. ("The Grave-Digger," *Lunacy and Letters*)

R

rabble: the people when the people are undemocratic. ("The Grave-Digger," *Lunacy and Letters*)

racism: anthropology gone mad; everlastingly looking for your own countrymen in other people's countries; the tribe on the march. ("The Heresy of Race," *The End of the Armistice*; *Illustrated London News*, Feb. 10, 1934)

radical: to be concerned with the root. (*Daily News*, Jan. 19, 1907)

Radical: a man who is convinced that the wrong is in the root of the system, and must be uprooted; a man who thinks things so bad that they require something as bad as a revolution to cure them. (*Daily News*, Mar. 11, 1911)

radio: a central mechanism giving out to men exactly what their masters think they should have. ("Babies and Distributism," *The Well and the Shallows*)

rain: a public bath; multitudinous cups of cold water handed round to all living things. ("The Romantic in the Rain," *A Miscellany of Men*)

Rationalism: free thought used to deny the existence of free will; the method by which a man detaches his brain from himself and lets it run alone. The Rationalist cuts his own head off and locks it up in a box. Then with the rest of himself he goes about his business, eating, drinking, working, fighting, falling in love. Then he comes back in the evening, opens the box, finds out what conclusions his head has come to, and accepts them. (*Illustrated London News*, Sep. 15, 1923; *Daily News*, Jan. 6, 1906)

Rationalist: an irrationalist. It is his interpretation of rationalism not merely to ask for the reason of things, but to refuse to see the things so long as he cannot see the reason. (*Illustrated London News*, Apr. 20, 1918)

Reactionary: a man one generation behind in the general disillusion about the last discovery; one in whom weariness itself has become a form of energy. (*Illustrated London News*, Apr. 19, 1924; "The Return of the Romans," *The Resurrection of Rome*)

reality: things attested to by the Authority of the Senses; a thing in which we can all repose, even if it hardly seems related to anything else. ("The Approach to Thomism," *St. Thomas Aquinas*; "The Man in the Cave," *The Everlasting Man*)

Realism: Romanticism that has lost its reason, that is, its reason for existing; the art of connecting everything that is in its nature disconnected; art in which dullness is relieved by horror or sometimes decorated with dirt. ("On Gargoyles," *Alarms and Discursions*; *Illustrated London News*, Mar. 12, 1910; Nov. 2, 1935)

realist: one who throws enough mud until some of it sticks, especially to that unfortunate creature Man, who was originally made of mud. (*Illustrated London News*, Mar. 12, 1910)

reason: the authority of man to think. ("The Suicide of Thought," *Orthodoxy*)

reasonable: defined. (*Daily News*, Nov. 2, 1912)

reform: altering the thing even in order to keep it the same; to see a certain thing out of shape and to put it into shape. And to know what shape. (*Daily News*, Aug. 24, 1907; "The Eternal Revolution, *Orthodoxy*)

Relativism: an irritation against all existing standards and ideals; the philosophy that there shall be no definable moral codes for the society of the future. (*Daily News*, June 2, 1906)

religion: something that commits a man to some doctrine about the universe; the sense of ultimate reality, of whatever meaning a man finds in his own existence or the existence of anything else; that which puts first things first; the power which makes us joyful about the things that matter; the responsible reinforcement of courage and common sense; a maid-of-all-work: a cosmic theory, a code of conduct, a system of artistic symbols, a fountain of fascinating tales; the telescope through which we can see the star upon which we dwell. ("The Angry Author: His Farewell," *A Miscellany of Men*; *Illustrated London News*, June 15, 1929; Apr. 26, 1930; "The Frivolous Man," *The Common Man*; "Five-Hundred-and-Fifty-Five," *Alarms and Discursions*; *Daily News*, Oct. 23, 1909; Introduction to *The Defendant*)

religious liberty: in theory, that everybody is free to discuss religion; in practice, that hardly anybody is allowed to mention it. ("The Shadow of the Sword," *Autobiography*)

republic: the Public Thing; the abstraction which is us all; the almost sacramental idea of representation, by which the few may incarnate the many. (*Illustrated London News*, Sep. 29, 1906; "The Other Kind of Man," *A Miscellany of Men*)

research: the search of people who don't know what they want. (*New Witness*, Oct. 14, 1915)

resolutions: virile and creative hopes. (*Illustrated London News*, Jan. 3, 1920)

retort: the cry of a man hit. (*The Bookman*, Oct. 1902)

revenge: a morbid personal perversion or poisoning of the eternal idea of justice. (*G.K.'s Weekly*, Nov. 12, 1927)

revolution: a rolling backward, a reversion to the natural and the normal; the act of doing without all the existing politicians; the mastering of matter by the spirit of man; the emergence of the human authority within us. ("Elizabeth Barrett Browning," *Varied Types*; *Illustrated London News*, Dec. 9, 1916; "The Free Man," *A Miscellany of Men*)

rhetoric: verbal form and verbal effect. ("The War with the Great Republics," *Short History of England*)

right: a quaint old Catholic conception. Formerly supposed to be the opposite of wrong. (*Time's Abstract and Brief Chronicle*)

ritual: ceremony, the object of which is not to be beautiful, though that is a valuable element, but the object of a ceremony is to be ceremonious; a need of the human soul—nay, it is rather a need of the human body, like exercise. (*Illustrated London News,* May 19, 1906)

rivalry: the war between two things, not because they are different but because they are alike. ("The Return of the Romans," *The Resurrection of Rome*)

romance: life felt as somebody feels it; the need for that mixture of the familiar and the unfamiliar; the natural kinship between war and wooing; the mood in literature that combines to the keenest extent the idea of danger and the idea of hope.

RIVALRY

(*Illustrated London News*, Mar. 17, 1906; Introduction to *Orthodoxy*; "Nicholas Nickleby," *Appreciations and Criticisms*; *Manchester Guardian*, May 18, 1914)

romantic: the real feelings of real and recognizable human beings. ("If Don John of Austria had Married Mary Queen of Scots," *The Common Man*)

S

sacrament: something that, though it is spiritual, it is also solid; certain and incredible; a materialized mystery. (*Illustrated London News*, Jan. 10, 1914; "The Strange Lady, *The Ball and the Cross*; *American Review*, Sept., 1935)

sacrifice: the destruction of the most precious thing for the glory of the divine powers; a guarantee against arrogance; a thing very deep in humanity indeed, the idea of surrendering something as the portion of the unknown powers; of pouring out wine upon the ground, of throwing a ring into the sea; the wise and worthy idea of not taking our advantage to the full; of putting something in the other balance to ballast our dubious pride, of paying tithes to nature for our land. This deep truth of the danger of insolence, or being too big for our boots, runs through all the great Greek tragedies and makes them great. Where that gesture of surrender is most magnificent, as among the great Greeks, there is really much more idea that the man will be the better for losing the ox than that the god will be the better for getting it. (*Illustrated London News*, Dec. 24, 1927; April 18, 1914; "Man and Mythologies," *The Everlasting Man*)

salesmanship: the culture of cads. (*G.K.'s Weekly*, Jan. 14, 1932)

salt: a corrective; something which we cannot live on, but cannot live without. (*Illustrated London News*, Oct. 30, 1915)

salvation: the great business of the soul. ("Rabelaisian Regrets," *The Common Man*)

sanity: tragedy in the heart and comedy in the head; free will. ("The Travellers in State," *Tremendous Trifles*; *Daily News*, May 14, 1904)

satire: the art of perceiving some absurdity inherent in the logic of some position and drawing that absurdity out and isolating it so that all can see it; the habit of treating people as if there were nothing about them except their opinions. ("Martin Chuzzlewit," *Appreciations*)

satirist: the man who carries men's enthusiasm further than they carry it themselves and sees where men's detached intellect will eventually lead them, and he tells them the name of the place—which is generally hell. ("Martin Chuzzlewit," *Appreciations*)

savage: a person who, like a modern artist, is driven to create something uglier than himself, though the artist finds it harder; a person with such an extraordinary inequality in the mind that he laughs when he hurts you and howls when you hurt him. (*Illustrated London News*, Nov. 25, 1905; "The Refusal of Reciprocity," *The Appetite of Tyranny*)

scandal: tripping somebody up, putting a stumbling-block in the way of some struggling human being. ("Some of Our Errors," *The Thing*)

scholarship: ignorance militant and triumphant. (*Illustrated London News*, Nov. 6, 1920)

science: the study of the admitted laws of existence, which cannot prove a universal negative about whether those laws could ever be suspended by something admittedly above them;

a vast design for producing accidents. ("Inge vs. Barnes," *The Thing*; *New Witness*, Oct. 14, 1915)

scientific method: a method not only of many experiments but of many failures. (*New Witness*, Feb. 24, 1916)

sea: the oldest and most unchangeable of all things. (*Illustrated London News*, Oct. 14, 1905)

secular: to be of the age; that is, of the age which is passing; of the age which, in the case of the secularists, is already passed. There is one tolerably correct translation of the Latin word which they have chosen as their motto. It does not mean anything so sensible as "worldly." It does not even mean anything so spirited as "irreligious." There is one adequate equivalent of the word "secular"; and it is the word "dated." ("My Six Conversions," *The Well and the Shallows*)

secularism: the idea that the religious sentiment, which stretched from one end of history to the other, is one vast hereditary malady and unbroken nightmare. (*Daily News*, June 18, 1901)

self-denial: the test and definition of self-government. ("The Field of Blood," *Alarms and Discursions*)

self-government: self-organization of a whole society from below. (*Illustrated London News*, Nov. 17, 1923)

self-made men: cads without a creator. ("At Overroads Door," *Return to Chesterton*)

self-pity: an evil that comes when a man thinks himself so very miserable a sinner that his misery is more important than his sin. (*Illustrated London News*, July 31, 1909)

self-sacrifice: making oneself sacred by dedicating oneself to some great thing of whose greatness one will henceforth partake. (*Daily News*, Dec. 21, 1912)

self-taught man: a man taught, not by himself, but by other people, by other people acting as they really act in the real world, and not as they pose before pupils they are paid to teach, a man taught by books rather than school-books. ("Tale of Two Cities," *The Common Man*)

sense: the quality whereby we become conscious of the presence of something; the receptiveness or approachability by the facts outside us. (*Daily News*, Feb.18, 1902; "Dickens and America," *Charles Dickens*)

senses: the channels of the first essential, direct and untainted information of the universe; the five great gates of God. (*Daily News*, Feb.18, 1902)

sentiment: that frame of mind in which all men admit, with a half-humorous and half-magnanimous weakness, that they all possess the same secret, and have all made the same discovery; a conventional term of abuse to be applied to Catholicism. (*The Speaker*, July 27, 1901; "The Hat and the Halo," *The Thing*)

sentimentalism: the indulgence of sympathetic emotions for their own sake, without application in social use, or reference to reality; a sin that only occurs when somebody indulges a feeling, sometimes even a real feeling, to the prejudice of something equally real, which also has its rights. (*G.K.'s Weekly*, Feb. 4, 1933; *Illustrated London News*, Aug. 20, 1927)

sentimentalist: simply a man who has feelings and does not trouble to invent a new way of expressing them; one who seeks to enjoy every idea without its sequence, and every pleasure without its consequence. ("A Defence of Penny Dreadfuls," *The Defendant*; "The Sentimentalist," *Alarms and Discursions*)

serious: a word of double-meaning and double-dealing, a traitor in the dictionary, that sometimes means solemn, and sometimes means sincere. ("The Philosopher," *George Bernard Shaw*)

seriousness: idolatry; a spirit that cannot even rouse itself enough to laugh. (*Illustrated London News*, Oct. 9, 1909; Sept. 29, 1923)

Servile State: a condition in which the law enforces labor upon a defined number of people, and guarantees the surplus wealth, or profit, of that labor as the private property of another and equally defined number of people. (*The New Statesman*, June 17, 1916)

Sesquipedalianism: the name of my new movement, which, incorporating in itself the converging forces of all modern movements, embodying all that the real modern spirit values in its various schemes and hopes, cannot but be the final concentrated concentric collectivity, into which all these approximate and relativistic collectivities will be sociologically coordinated. (*New York American*, Mar. 4, 1933)

sex: the great business of the body. ("Rabelaisian Regrets," *The Common Man*)

shyness: the comic form of humility. ("Our Mutual Friend," *Appreciations and Criticisms*)

siege: a peace plus the inconvenience of war. ("The Great Army of South Kensington," *The Napoleon of Notting Hill*)

SERIOUSNESS

sin: the wrong use of the will; the only part of Christian theology which can really be proved. ("The Outline of the Fall," *The Thing*; "The Maniac," *Orthodoxy*)

skeptic: a man who praises the hardness of his head because it keeps out common sense; a person who makes his personality the only test, instead of making truth the test; one who has seen and yet disbelieved. (*Illustrated London News*, Jan. 12, 1929; May 4, 1907; *Daily News*, May 20, 1905)

skepticism: a dogma of hopelessness and definite belief in unbelief; an absurd assumption that a man is in some way just and well-poised because he has come to no conclusion. ("The Progressive," *George Bernard Shaw*; *Illustrated London News*, May 4, 1907)

sketch: an affair of a few lines. ("Later Life and Works," *Charles Dickens*)

skirt: a thing that falls with artistic freedom, that can be lifted or kissed like the robes of the old prophets, that can sweep the ground like the trains of Pontiffs and kings. (*Illustrated London News*, April 13, 1911)

sky: the serene arch of infinity. ("The Yellow Bird," *The Poet and the Lunatics*)

slander: a confession of the supreme importance of morality. (*Illustrated London News*, Oct. 5, 1907)

slang: the apparent distortion of a dialect; a constantly changing game or practical joke with the language; that normal popular habit of taking liberties with language; the one stream of poetry which is continually flowing. (*New York American*, Aug. 10, 1935; *G.K.'s Weekly*, May 9, 1931; "A Defence of Slang," *The Defendant*)

slavery: the owning of a man's body as one owns a tool. (*Illustrated London News*, Aug. 1, 1908)

sleep: a mysterious pleasure which is too perfect to be remembered, some forgotten refreshment at the ancient fountains of life; a sacrament, or, what is the same thing, a food. ("On Keeping a Dog," *Lunacy and Letters*)

snobbery: the religion of the irreligious. (*Illustrated London News*, Jan. 13, 1913)

social evolution: the theory that true progress consists in doing everything as slowly as possible, and letting everything slide into everything else, on the same principle by which a dissipated club-man becomes an apostle of early rising and a simple diet by the mere act of coming home with the milk; the victory of the man who can afford to wait. (*New Witness*, Oct. 5, 1916; *Daily News*, Nov. 17, 1906)

social service: slavery without loyalty; the sinister motto of the heathen Servile State; the labour of numberless and nameless men, toiling like ants and dying like flies, wiped out by the work of their own hands. ("A Summary," *The Outline of Sanity*; "The Antiquity of Civilization," *The Everlasting Man*)

Socialism: the ownership by the organ of government (whatever it is) of all things necessary to production; the theory that the State is the only absolute in morals—that is, that there is no appeal from it to God or man, to Christendom or conscience, to the individual or the family or the fellowship of all mankind; the pretence that government can prevent all injustice by being directly responsible for practically anything that happens; the fallacy that there is an absolutely unlimited number of inspired officials and an absolutely unlimited amount of money to pay them; a form of Manicheanism that castrates men to keep them pure. ("The Sectarian of Society," *A Miscellany of Men*; *Illustrated London News*, Dec. 22, 1918; Oct. 10, 1925; *The Listener,* Nov. 27, 1935; *Platitudes Undone*)

Socialist: a man not bold and logical enough to call himself a Communist; a person who believes that the monstrous division of modern property can only be cured by the Government, the State, coming in and coercively claiming all the property and paying it back in wages to the citizens. (*G.K.'s Weekly*, Jan. 30, 1936; Debate with Shaw, Nov. 30, 1911)

sociology: the modern attempt to combine wild spiritual speculation with systematic scientific order in order to explain that men were united by religions and loyalties, and then widely scattered. (*Illustrated London News*, April 25, 1931)

Sophist: a type of man, a very ancient and irritating type, a type known to Socrates and well known to us, whose peculiarity is this, that by mere intellectual ingenuity he disproves at once all the things which ordinary and honest men know to be noble and all the things which ordinary and sensible men know to be true. (*Daily News*, April 2, 1904)

sophistry: the untruthful selection of truths; a mere ingenious defense of the indefensible. (*Illustrated London News*, May 13, 1916; Introduction to *Orthodoxy*)

soul: the unknown quantity in man; something that can sin and that can sacrifice itself. (*Daily News*, Mar. 1, 1901, "The Field of Blood," *Alarms and Discursions*)

Spiritualism: a mere mixing up of the two sacred nations of the living and the dead; a trend of polytheism in a form more akin to ancestor-worship. Whether it be the invocation of ghosts or of gods, the mark of it is that it invokes something less than the divine. (*New Witness*, Dec. 2, 1915; "The Other Side of the Desert," *The New Jerusalem*)

Spiritualist: a man whose religion consists entirely of ghosts. (*Illustrated London News*, May 30, 1936)

sport: a frivolous thing taken seriously. (*Illustrated London News*, Aug. 25, 1906)

squire: the tadpole of Knighthood. ("The Meaning of Merry England," *A Short History of England*)

statistician: someone trying to make a rigid and unchangeable chain out of elastic links. (*Illustrated London News*, July 23, 1927)

stick: the scepter of man; the wooden pillar of his house; a piece of our ancient civilization especially in this; that it is a universal thing, and has many functions. It is sometimes a crutch, sometimes a club, sometimes a balancing pole, sometimes a mere toy to twiddle in the fingers. Sometimes it is used for holding a man up, and sometimes for knocking him down. (*Daily News*, Oct. 23, 1910)

story: something that ends differently than it began. ("The Escape from Paganism," *The Everlasting Man*)

strangers: those who need an introduction. ("Miracles and Death," *St. Francis of Assisi*)

suburb: a nondescript neutral territory which grows up just outside the wall of the city on the spot which older and wiser civilizations reserved entirely for the execution of criminals; the indefinite expansion controlled neither by the soul of the city from within, nor by the resistance of the lands round about; a thing that destroys at once the dignity of a town and

SPORT

the freedom of a countryside. (*New York American*, Feb. 11, 1933; "The Gates of the City," *The New Jerusalem*)

subjective: <u>a word used by the moderns when they mean false.</u> ("Man and Mythologies," *The Everlasting Man*)

suggestion: appeal to the irrational part of man. (*Illustrated London News*, Oct. 11, 1930)

suicide: the ultimate and absolute evil, the refusal to take an interest in existence; the refusal to take the oath of loyalty to life; the murder of the only man whose happiness we can appreciate. ("The Flag of the World," *Orthodoxy*; *Daily News*, Dec. 13, 1901)

Superman: whatever creature happens to find itself on top of man. (*Illustrated London News*, Dec. 19, 1908)

supernatural: all the things higher and holier than mankind. (*G.K.'s Weekly*, July 5, 1934)

superstition: a belief that is held without knowing any reason for it; a sort of somber fairy-tale that we tell to ourselves in order to express the mystery of the strange laws of life; the creative side of agnosticism. (*The Superstitions of the Sceptic; Illustrated London News*, May 28, 1910; "Ibsen," *A Handful of Authors*)

surprise: the secret of joy; the only real happiness, the only kind of reflection that is possible to man. (*Illustrated London News*, Dec. 11, 1922; "The Pickwick Papers," *Charles Dickens*)

sympathy: not so much feeling with all who feel, but rather suffering with all who suffer. ("The Great Victorian Novelists," *Victorian Age in Literature*)

symposium: the old Greek title that has fallen from its first

SUPERMAN

high classical purity and dignity of meaning, by which it meant drinks all round, and descended—nay, degenerated—until it only means a set of separate printed statements, generally in every sense dry. (*Illustrated London News*, April 2, 1932)

T

teetotaler: one who is inspired and intoxicated by the absence of beer. (*Illustrated London News*, Feb. 10, 1934)

telegram: a dart that writes. ("The Romance of Machinery," *The Outline of Sanity*)

telemarketing: a sort of acoustic house-breaking, by which the man on whom we should always shut the outer door could yet appear in the inner chamber. (*Illustrated London News*, Feb. 10, 1923)

telephone: an instrument by which I can talk to a man across England when I have nothing worth saying even to a man next door. (*Daily News*, Jan. 5, 1907)

television: a barbarous and monstrous word, which is a horrible mongrel muddle of Greek and Latin, made up by someone who knew neither. (*New York American*, Mar. 5, 1932) (see also radio)

temperance: the intemperate denunciation of temperate drinking. ("On Courage and Independence," *The Thing*)

terrorists: well-meaning people engaged in the task, so obviously ultimately hopeless, of using science to promote morality. ("On Negative Morality," *Heretics*)

thanks: the highest form of thought. ("The Age of the Crusades," *A Short History of England*)

theatre: a festival where crowds may gather and sing the praise of life. The theatre is nothing if it is not joyful; the theatre is nothing if it is not sensational; the theatre is nothing if it is not theatrical. A play may be happy, it may be sad, it may be wild, it may be quiet, it may be tragic, it may be comic, but it must be festive. It must be something which works men up to a point, something which is passionate and abrupt and exceptional, something which makes them feel that they have in reality got a shilling's worth of emotion. It must be a festival. It must be a "treat." If it is a treat, a festival, it matters nothing whether it is comic or tragic, realistic or idealistic, Ibsenite or Rostandesque, happy or pitiful: it is a play. (*Daily News*, Jan. 17, 1902)

theft: a confession of our dependence on society. ("Oliver Twist," *Appreciations*)

theology: the element of reason in religion; the reason that prevents it from being a mere emotion; simply that part of religion that requires brains. ("The Hat and the Halo," *The Thing*; *Platitudes Undone*)

thinking: a kind of work which any man can do, but from which many men shrink, generally because it is very hard work, sometimes because they fear it will lead them whither they do not wish to go; loyalty to truth; connecting things. (*Illustrated London News*, July 10, 1915; May 27, 1911; "The Suicide of Thought," *Orthodoxy*)

thought: the attempt to discover if one's own conception is true or not. (*Platitudes Undone*)

thoughtlessness: a habit of beginning a sentence without apparently knowing or caring how it is going to end. (*Illustrated London News*, Apr. 27, 1912)

thrift: making the most of everything. (*Illustrated London News*, June 29, 1935)

tiger: a large cat that took the prize (and the prize-giver) and escaped to the jungle. ("The Other Side of the Desert," *The New Jerusalem*)

tolerance: barbaric indifference instead of civilized synthesis. (*Dublin Review*, Oct. 1910)

tool: something that does not know why it is a tool. (*Illustrated London News*, Mar. 17, 1917)

torture: forcing speech by inflicting pain, or threatening to inflict it; the enormous secret cruelty that has crowned every historic civilization, which has always been most artistic and elaborate when everything else was most artistic and elaborate. (*Illustrated London News*, Feb. 4, 1928; "The Travellers in State," *Tremendous Trifles*)

Tosh: (sometimes pronounced Bosh, and by Americans, Bunk) an explanation, which does not explain, of something which is explained already. (*New York American*, Sept. 16, 1933)

tourist: the sort of man who admires Italian art while despising Italian religion. ("Roman Converts," *Dublin Review*, Jan–Mar. 1925)

trade: to buy things for less than their worth and sell them for more than their worth. (*Dublin Review*, Jan–Mar, 1925)

traders: men who cannot do anything else except exchange; who have not the wits or the force or fancy or freedom of mind or even the humor and patience to bring anything into existence; who can only barter and bargain and generally cheat, with the things that manlier men have made. (*G.K.'s Weekly*, Jan. 14, 1933)

tradition: the truth of the common people; a sacred subconsciousness; a dark kinship and brotherhood of all mankind which is much too deep to be called heredity or to be in any way explained in scientific formulae; experience surviving death; democracy extended through time; giving votes to the most obscure of all classes, our ancestors; the democracy of the dead. (*Illustrated London News*, Sept. 18, 1926; "Christmas Books," *Appreciations*; *G.K.'s Weekly*, April 25, 1935; "The Ethics of Elfland," *Orthodoxy*.)

traffic: everybody making the same mistake at the same moment. (*Illustrated London News*, April 6, 1935)

tragedy: the highest expression of the infinite value of human life; the point when things are left to God and men can do no more. ("The Twelve Men," *Tremendous Trifles*; "Vanity Fair," *A Handful of Authors*)

traitor: the man who can live by anything, but for nothing. (*Daily News*, Jan. 8, 1902)

transcendent: a weak and vague word used in modern philosophy; it means a thing is only something that may be more something than something else that has not been defined. It sounds fiercely attractive. (*Daily News*, Dec. 15, 1906)

transparency: a sort of transcendental color. ("The Crime of Gabriel Gale," *The Poet and the Lunatics*)

Traveling Salesman: a person who goes to see people because they don't want to see him. ("The Sentimentalist," *Alarms and Discursions*)

treason: the greatest, or, at the very least, one of the greatest, of all conceivable sins, which consists in first establishing or recognizing a certain relation with a certain thing and then presuming on that relation to betray it to the enemy; the renunciation of the ancient loyalties, the cowardice which recoils from the great perils of affection, and incapacity for devotion of any kind, a timorous and panic-stricken independence. (*Daily News*, Jan. 28, 1903; Jan. 8, 1902)

tree: a top-heavy monster with a hundred arms, a thousand tongues, and only one leg . . . and no dogmas. ("Science and the Savages," "Concluding Remarks," *Heretics*)

trousers: a skirt on each leg. ("The Coldness of Chloe," *What's Wrong with the World*)

truism: a dead truth, a truth that we no longer feel as true. (*The Speaker*, Sept. 14, 1901)

truth: a fact with meaning; a living fact; a fact that can talk; a fact that is conscious of other facts; a fact that can explain itself. (*Illustrated London News*, Nov. 18, 1905; *Daily News*, July 2, 1910)

Tympanomania: a morbid craving to walk behind a big drum. (*Illustrated London News*, Mar. 30, 1907)

Tyrannicide: a devil that can cast out devils. (*Illustrated London News*, April 13, 1907)

tyranny: any kind of force used so as to override the natural rights of another person; a system to deal with men in herds; to treat them like sheep; and not only to class them with the beasts that perish but to take particular care that they do perish. (*Daily News,* April 1, 1911; *Illustrated London News*, July 7, 1934)

U

undertaker: a euphemism, and not a very wholesome one; It means that we need not think about such things, because there is some slave who will undertake It—that is, who will take It away. (*New Witness*, Jan. 20, 1916)

umbrella: an unmanageable walking stick and an inadequate tent. ("The Romantic in the Rain," *A Miscellany of Men*)

Universalism: a sort of optimistic Calvinism. ("The Crime of Orthodoxy," *Autobiography*)

universe: the supreme example of a thing that is too obvious to be seen. (*The Superstitions of the Sceptic*)

Unsectarianism: a sect—and a small sect; a fixed, very formal, and slightly hypocritical creed that talks of not caring for creeds. (*Illustrated London News*, Nov. 14, 1908)

usurer: one who lends the poor that funny cash that makes them poorer still. ("Song of the Strange Ascetic," *Wine, Water and Song*)

utopia: a fixed perfection on this planet, with men at leisure and machines in labor, that is untraditional and unhistorical. (*New Witness*, Sept. 30, 1921; *G.K.'s Weekly*, April 25, 1935)

V

vaccination: destroying a disease by doling it out in very small quantities. (*Daily News*, Nov. 2, 1912)

valor: putting one's full value into the struggle; the almost exact translation is "being in it for all you are worth." (*Daily News*, Dec. 12, 1908)

UMBRELLA

vandalism: the brutal destruction of beauty. (*New York American*, June 4, 1932)

vanity: a desire for praise. (*Illustrated London News*, Nov. 12, 1910)

Vegetarianism: the belief that the body is a sort of magical factory where things go in as vegetables and come out as virtues; the only religion on earth that has in it no agnosticism and no humility. ("The Meaning of Mock Turkey," *Fancies vs. Fads*; *Illustrated London News*, April 28, 1906)

villain: a ceaseless, ruthless, and uncompromising menace. ("On the Alleged Optimism of Dickens," *Charles Dickens*)

vindictiveness: the desire to hurt somebody who has hurt us. (*Illustrated London News*, Feb. 3, 1917)

virtue: a duty that one can't do; something that does some good to everybody. ("The School for Hypocrites," *What's Wrong with the World*, "The Church of the Servile State," *Utopia of Usurers*)

vote: the power of the people to make a Government in their own image, to control the general atmosphere of their own affairs, and to make or unmake laws in the light of their own experience of how laws affect them. (*Illustrated London News*, April 25, 1914)

voting: governing in council; an attempt to get at the opinion of those who would be too modest to offer it. (*Illustrated London News*, May 19, 1906; "The Eternal Revolution," *Orthodoxy*)

vow: a tryst with oneself; to combine the fixity that goes with finality with the self-respect that only goes with freedom. (Part I, Part VI, *The Superstition of Divorce*)

VULGAR

vulgar: laughing loudly to prove that one has no sense of humor; being tactful without tact; showing off to show how little one has to show. (*Illustrated London News*, June 8, 1929)

vulgarity: having at once familiarity and insensibility; handling things confidently and contemptuously, without the sense that all things in their way are sacred things. ("Culture and the Coming Peril," Speech delivered June 28, 1927; "Vulgarity," *The Common Man*)

W

war: the awful game of saving the State by violence; the idea of a positive fight against a positive evil. (*New Witness*, Dec. 23, 1915; *Illustrated London News*, Mar. 21, 1914)

waste: a kind of murder, a merely negative and destructive thing, the obliteration of something which we can neither value nor understand. ("A Sermon on Cheapness," *The Apostle and the Wild Ducks*)

water: a medicine. It should be taken in small quantities in very extreme cases; as when one is going to faint. (*Illustrated London News*, May 21, 1910)

wealth: a fog which always obscures realities. (*G.K.'s Weekly*, Dec. 17, 1927)

weariness: the inaction of one who fails to act as he would otherwise like to act. (*Illustrated London News*, Aug. 25, 1917)

whale: a cow that went swimming and never came back. ("The Other Side of the Desert," *The New Jerusalem*)

whitewashing: the hiding or hushing up of political or financial scandals and similar things; the contrary and the copy of washing; using purity to conceal impurity instead of removing impurity to reveal purity. (*New York American*, Sept. 3, 1935)

will: the choice of something, but the rejection of almost everything. ("The Suicide of Thought," *Orthodoxy*)

window: a thing which admits light. (*Daily News*, Jan. 17, 1902)

wine: one of the few really inspiring arguments for vegetarianism. (*Illustrated London News*, Dec. 19, 1908)

wise few: either the few whom the foolish think wise or the very foolish who think themselves wise. ("The Priest of Spring," *A Miscellany of Men*)

wit: instantaneous presence of mind; human intellect exerting its full strength, though perhaps upon a small point; reason on its judgment seat; a sword meant to make people feel the point as well as see it. ("The Sequel to St. Thomas," *St. Thomas Aquinas*; "Humour," *The Spice of Life*; "Mark Twain,," *A Handful of Authors*)

witch: somebody who has made a contract with Satan. (*Illustrated London News*, Dec. 6, 1913)

wonder: the beginning of worship; the soul of all the arts. (*New Witness*, April 16, 1916; "Belfast and the Religious Problem," *Irish Impressions*)

wood: the most human of non-human things. (*New Witness*, Oct. 26, 1916)

word: a verbal symbol. (*Illustrated London News*, June 8, 1929)

work: doing what you do not like. ("Tommy and the Traditions," *Lunacy and Letters*)

workers: men mostly out of work. (*G.K.'s Weekly*, Oct. 11, 1934)

worldly wisdom: a bewildering whirlpool of platitudes and half truths. (*Daily News*, Jan. 14, 1905)

XYZ

x: the unknown quantity, which may have a meaning, as it does in Xmas. (*Illustrated London News*, Nov. 10, 1934)

yawn: a silent yell. ("The Philosopher," *George Bernard Shaw*)

Yo: the thing by which the skeptics, in seeking to escape the dilemma of the everlasting duel between Yes and No, have darkened the universe and dissolved the mind by trying to maintain that there is something that is both Yes and No. ("The Permanent Philosophy," *St. Thomas Aquinas*)

young: that which has life before it. (*Illustrated London News*, Nov. 18, 1911)

youth: the period of irresponsibility. ("Charles Dickens: His Life," *Encyclopaedia Britannica*,1929)

zero: dark nothingness. ("Le Jongleur de Dieu," *St. Francis of Assisi*)

—compiled by Dale Ahlquist and John Peterson